Wahida Clark Presents Publishing
60 Evergreen Place
Suite 904A
East Orange, New Jersey 07018
973-678-9982
www.wclarkpublishing.com

Library of Congress Cataloging-In-Publication Data:
Alah Adams
American D-Boy
ISBN 13-digit 978-19366491-6-7 (paper)
ISBN 10-digit   1936649160 (paper)
ISBN (ebook) 978-1-936649-53-2
LCCN: 2014916298

1. New York- 3. Drug Trafficking- 4. African American-Fiction- 5. Urban Fiction- 6. Street gangs- 7. D-Boy

Cover design and layout by Nuance Art, LLC
Book design by NuanceArt@aCreativeNuance.com
Edited by Linda Wilson
Proofreader Rosalind Hamilton

Printed in USA

ALAH ADAMS

To Yolanda
Thank you sister
Enjoy

(signature)

AMERICAN D-BOY

Special Thanks

First and foremost I want to thank the Creative Forces of the Universe for allowing me to exist. Second I want to thank my parents for guiding me in the right direction. Last but not least I want to thank Mrs. Wahida Clark for believing in me and treating me like a brother. I also want to thank Linda Wilson, one of the best editors in the game.

My children, Alah Jr., Dejour, Elijah, and my little princess Audrey. These four people inspire me more than anyone on the earth! My beautiful Queen Lisa is my rock that held me down when things got rough. My Mother for being patient with me and believing that I'd make it one day.

When I started writing this book I didn't know exactly where I was going with it. My team, Shoota, N.I., and Sha gave me so much direction without them even knowing it. They were just being themselves and they inspired me. Thanks for being Hood, Gangster, and most of all loyal.

This has been a long journey that was well worth it. I didn't chose writing, writing chose me. Now that I've accepted the challenge, I'm headed for the top of this game! What I write is heavily influenced by Hip Hop culture. That being said, I want to dedicate this book to Hip Hop. Hip Hop music began with the DJ. One of my favorite DJ's of all time was Jam Master Jay. He was the most gangster DJ in the history of Hip Hop. That's why one of my main characters is named Jason and he became a DJ.

R.I.P. JAM MASTER JAY!

ALAH ADAMS

There's more to come! Stay tuned!
–Alah Adams

ALAH ADAMS

AMERICAN D-BOY!

Written by

ALAH ADAMS

ALAH ADAMS

AMERICAN D-BOY

PROLOGUE

JAMAICA ESTATES
Jamaica Queens, New York

Jamaica Estates was a prestigious community lined with mini-palatial mansions, immaculate manicured lawns, and a middle-aged Caucasian man in hiding. The bushes aligning the front and the sides created natural-like fences that concealed the six-foot-tall vagrant with wild, sandy brown hair and an unkempt full beard. Normally, it was a quiet neighborhood, not many people walking on the street. That's also why no one noticed the bum lying under the bushes of house number 216.

He lay there clad in Levi's and a dirty brown burlap trench coat that covered a filthy white T-shirt. Patiently he waited. And just like clockwork, his mark exited the house and got into the pearly white Mercedes Benz parked in the driveway. Then he started it up.

"Good riddance, you rat bastard!" The bum pressed the red button on the remote control device in his hand.

"BOOM!"

The explosion was so deafening the bum's ears were ringing like the Liberty Bell. The bomb exploded the CLS 63 AMG Mercedes from the inside, engulfing the interior. Ironically, all of the windows and doors were intact. D-Boy had the entire car double reinforced with steel, making it not only bulletproof, but bomb-proof as well—that was, *if* the bomb was on the outside of the car. Unfortunately, someone planted the bomb under the driver's seat, so the body was trapped inside and blown to bits.

"Time to get the fuck outta here!" the bum said.

Right before he made a move to leave his hiding spot, an unmarked FBI vehicle was pulling up, so he quickly got back under the bush. Two plain clothes agents got out and walked next to the bush. They had arrived so fast because they were already on the block waiting to tail D-Boy. When they heard the bomb, they knew it came from D-Boy's house.

"Damn! I didn't even get the chance to send him off with a swift kick in his ass. I hated that nigger. I'm kind of glad he's finally out of his misery," Agent Trenton said to his junior partner, Agent Kowalski.

"Now we can't put those charges on him. I know how bad you wanted to see him rot in jail for what he did to Steph," Agent Kowalski commented.

"Oh well, let's call the fire department to see if they can't get this fire under control before it burns down this beautiful house." Agent Trenton took his cell phone out and dialed 911.

The two agents were so close to the bum that he could see their feet. He tried not to breathe too hard, or make any sudden movement. They would have to kill him because he'd heard their whole conversation, so he lay as stiff as a mannequin. He knew if he didn't get out of there before the fire trucks and the NYPD arrived, he'd be discovered. He waited for the right moment to present itself. The agents finally got into their car, which gave him a chance to crawl to the backyard and hop the fence to safety. He ran as fast as he could, two blocks down, where a black SUV with tinted windows awaited him. Quickly, he took out the keys, unlocked the door, and drove off while the New York Fire Department was speeding toward the burning Mercedes Benz.

Later that afternoon, the Queens County Coroner's Office confirmed that the charred remains found in the Mercedes did indeed belong to one, Darius 'D-Boy' Jensen. The news of D-Boy's murder spread like wildfire. In just two hours the entire NYC knew about D-Boy's demise. Some rejoiced because they hated D-Boy, and others mourned because he helped several people financially. D-Boy paid rent for quite a few elderly people from his neighborhood. Nevertheless, D-Boy's murder was the end of a vast criminal empire, and the beginning of an unsettling mystery: Who killed D-Boy?

JOHNSON'S FUNERAL HOME
Queens, New York

Johnson's funeral home was wall to wall packed. People were standing in the aisles and on the front steps leading to the entrance. It wasn't every day that people had a chance to pay their respects to a street legend. It seemed as if the entire New York City came out to pay homage to Darius 'D-Boy' Jensen.

Twenty NYPD police officers stood in attendance to make sure nothing dangerous happened. D-Boy's funeral brought out all the gangsters, pimps, and drug dealers from NYC and all over the country. Even some members of the Italian and Russian Mafia came out to pay their respect to the young gangster.

D-Boy was murdered at the tender age of twenty-five years old. All that remained of his body were charred pieces of human bones and his skull. It was hard to pinpoint who was responsible because D-Boy made so many enemies on both sides of the fence. On one side, rival drug dealers wanted him dead because he was getting all the money. Then, Federal Agents wanted him dead because they couldn't pin him with enough evidence to put him away. All their star witnesses came up dead or missing, so they couldn't win in trial.

D-Boy didn't have a wife or kids. The only family he had was his older brother, Jason 'DJ Jay-Roc' Jenson, Grandpa Joe, and his father, OG Jesse Jensen. He did have over $25 million in cash stashed where only he and Jason were privy to. But money was the last thing on Jason's mind.

The funeral was a closed casket service, so a large picture of him sat upon an easel. Hundreds of people walked up to his casket and viewed his picture before heading out. D-Boy's artist and crony, Shoota, walked up and sat next to Jason. Shoota and D-Boy hadn't known each other that long, but D-Boy considered him a loyal friend.

"I can't believe he's gone," Shoota spoke in a somber tone.

Jason took a deep breath and replied, "That's my only brother. We didn't have any sisters. It was just me and D-Boy."

Grandpa Joe sat just to the right of Jason. "I never thought I'd live long enough to bury my grandson," he said while tears rolled down his cheeks.

"We all have to go sometime. It was just his time to go," D-Boy's father, OG Jesse whispered, holding back tears.

An hour later it was time to take D-Boy to his final destination. Six pallbearers took their positions to carry the gold casket to the hearse. Jason, Grandpa Joe, OG, and Shoota all got into a limousine and sat solemn on the way to the cemetery. Each man had their own personal memory of their fallen soldier.

When they arrived at the cemetery, many cars in their caravan couldn't make it into the burial area. Most vehicles just blocked traffic; you'd think a dignitary was being buried. It was definitely a funeral fit for a gangster with the likes of D-Boy.

"We are here to send Darius Jensen home to be with the one and only Father, God. He was a vibrant young man so full of life. It's a tragedy that he had to go so soon! But when God has a plan, no man can interfere with his design. When he calls you home you have no choice but to answer."

The pastor looked at all the young gangsters in attendance. They all wore hard expressions. "All of you young men here today need to learn a lesson from Darius's demise, and that's to stop the violence and stop living this life of crime! How many young men have to die? This epidemic of killing each other and destroying the community has to stop!" He paused and closed his eyes. "Let us bow our heads in prayer for Brother Darius Jensen. It's time to say our final farewells." Those words signaled the lowering of the casket into its six-foot-deep resting place.

While everyone bowed their heads, Jason was looking around and spotted a white man standing next to a tree in the distance looking right at him. When their gazes locked, he walked away. *That's strange,* Jason thought.

After D-Boy was in the ground, everyone departed except Jason, Grandpa Joe, OG Jesse and Shoota. They all stood around while the grounds keeper shoveled dirt onto the casket.

"I still can't believe he's gone. D-Boy was the realest nigga on earth!" Shoota said.

"Word! He was definitely the last of a dying breed. They don't make 'em like D-Boy anymore. These new ass niggas are fake as hell!" OG Jesse said, "And I'm not just saying that because he was my son. D-Boy was official tissue!"

Jason just smiled. He was the closest person to D-Boy, so he knew him very well. "There will never be another D-Boy," Jason said.

"I have to get out of here and go take care of some business. Are you coming, Jason?" OG Jesse asked.

"You guys go ahead. I'm going to stay here and meditate," Jason responded.

Everyone left the gravesite except Jason. He sat on the fresh cut grass next to D-Boy's burial plot and reminisced on the good old days when they were children. "Damn! I wish you would've just listened to me when I told you to leave the streets alone! None of that shit was worth it! You were finally ready to make a change, and then you were taken away just like that!" Jason released his anger.

The bum stood behind him listening. He wanted to approach Jason, but he didn't want to startle him while he was mourning. Slowly, he walked up and stood by Jason.

"How you doing, good brother? You wouldn't happen to have some change?" the bum asked humbly.

"Sure." Jason reached into his pocket and pulled out a dollar bill. "Here you go, brother." *That's the same bum that was standing in the distance watching me,* Jason thought.

"Is that your family they buried today?" the bum asked.

"Yes, that's the only brother I had. Now it's just me," Jason replied.

"Oh, I see. What did he die from? If you don't mind me asking."

"Someone blew up his car. He had it bullet-proofed, but his body burned to a crisp before they could finally get him out and put the fire out." Jason paused because the tears lumped up his throat. "I just wish we had a different up-bringing. Then maybe he wouldn't have gone that route."

"It sounds like you have a lot on your mind. I don't have nothing but time. If you want to talk I'm all ears."

A chill went up his spine while Jason reflected. "I remember how it all began, as if it was yesterday . . ."

CHAPTER 1

SIXTEEN YEARS AGO
South Side Jamaica Queens, New York

JASON

Jason Jensen was born and raised in South Side Jamaica, Queens. Everybody in his hood knew The Jensen Family. Not because there were a lot of them, only four men were left: Jason, his little brother Darius, their father OG Jesse, and Grandpa Joe. All four men called it a curse of the Jensen's. Jason and Darius's mother and grandmothers were deceased, and they had no other family members that they knew of.

The only reason The Jensen Family got respect in their hood was because of OG Jesse Jensen, who was one of the biggest heroin dealers from Queens. OG Jesse had been getting money in the streets since the early 80s, and that's how he got the OG in front of his name, which stood for Original Gangster.

Grandpa Joe and OG Jesse must've had strong genes because all the Jensen men had the same features, tall, light-skinned, and handsome. Their Native American blood mixed with their African American blood, resulted in naturally long, straight

16

hair that they kept braided. DNA aside, Jason and Darius also received great values and principals from their father, OG Jesse. He stepped up to raise both of his sons as a single father, which was uncommon for a hustler.

At the age of thirteen, OG Jesse bought Jason a turntable set for Christmas. That's all he did was mix and scratch records. Jason practiced until he was mixing and scratching records like a disc jockey prodigy.

One evening he stood in his room at the turntables instead of cracking open his books to finish his homework. His conscience worked him over, and so did the idea of his dad walking in and busting him. *I know I'm not supposed to mess with the turntables until my homework is done and I clean up my room, but an hour won't hurt.* Still, Jason turned the power on and stood his tall, lanky frame up to the turntables. He put his headphones on and went to work.

"I thought I told you no mixing until you clean up this pig sty of a room, and do your homework!" his father yelled as he entered the room. OG Jesse realized Jason couldn't hear him because of the headphones over his ears, so he snatched them off Jason's head and repeated his first command.

The action startled Jason, but he gave his dad his full attention. "Can I mix for just one hour? Please, Dad!" he pleaded.

"One hour, and then I want you cleaning up this room!"

OG Jesse made his exit, and then walked through the spacious house, stopping at Darius's room.

"Darius, make sure you do your homework too. You come home from school and all you do is play that damn game! How do you expect to pass to the fourth grade if you don't do the work?" he asked.

"Can I just finish this last level? Please, Dad!" Darius begged.

"One last game. Then I want to see you in those books." His cell phone began ringing. OG Jesse gave Darius a warning gaze before leaving his room.

"Where the hell is that damn cell phone?" He found it on the kitchen counter. "Hello?"

"What up, OG? This is Tone. I need to see you ASAP. Can I come to the crib?"

"Listen, I usually don't conduct business at my house, but I'm going to see you this one time," OG Jesse replied.

"Good looking, OG. You know you're good with me. I just need those new cakes."

"Call me when you're outside, and oh yeah, come by yourself." OG Jesse hung up.

Fifteen minutes later, Tone called. "What up, OG? I'm outside."

"Okay, walk up to my garage and wait."

OG Jessie entered the garage from a door inside the house. He took the 45-millimeter handgun that was hidden under a workbench and cocked it back. Once he took the safety off for a quick draw, he hid it on his waist. He stopped short before opening the garage and went back into the main house.

"Hey, Jason!" OG Jesse said. Jason didn't respond because he had headphones on. "Jason!" OG Jesse stood in front of Jason, getting his attention.

"Oh, what up, Dad?" Jason lowered the music and removed the headphones.

"I'm going into the garage to handle some business. Don't go in there until I'm done."

"Okay." Jason went back to doing what he loved most, spinning records on the wheels of steel.

Three minutes later, OG Jesse opened the garage, and to his surprise he saw two men and not one as instructed. "Who the fuck is this dude? I thought I told you to come alone!" he told Tone.

Before he could reach his weapon, Tone pushed him into the garage while his partner pulled out his gun and pointed it at OG Jesse's head. Tone entered, and then he closed the garage.

"Move real easy, OG. We don't have to make this messy, just give up the work and the money." Tone pulled out his weapon.

OG Jesse moved toward the back of the garage where his hidden stash spot was located. As he moved, his mind was racing. *I have to get to my gun. These amateurs didn't even check me for a weapon. I got a little surprise for them.*

As OG reached for gun, his nine-year-old son, Darius opened the garage door. "Hey Da—!" Darius tried to call out.

In that split second, Tone turned in Darius's direction and let off a shot. Darius's small body spun in a 180 degree circle before hitting the floor.

"Darius!" OG Jesse yelled.

Tone couldn't believe what he'd just done. "Damn! OG, I didn't mean to shoot him!"

OG Jesse didn't flinch when he pulled out his weapon, crouched low and fired four shots in rapid succession, all in one swift motion. Two shots hit Tone's accomplice in his chest and neck. He fell to the floor, blood spewing from his neck, and his chest had a hole in it the size of a grapefruit. He had minutes before the life force energy would drain from his body.

Tone was hit in his shoulder, causing him to drop his weapon. He stood by the garage with his one good arm in the air. "Please don't shoot me. It was all his plan. I don't even—" Before he could finish his sentence, OG Jesse pulled the trigger but nothing came out. His gun had jammed.

Everything was happening so fast, but OG Jesse had to make a move. He knew he had seconds to act, so he rushed to Darius's side and quickly found the wound and stopped the bleeding by applying pressure to the spot. At the same time he took out his cell phone and dialed 911.

"Please hurry to 394 Hawthorne Ave! My nine-year-old son has been shot in his chest! He has lost a lot of blood already! Please hurry!" OG Jesse was frantic.

While he was attending to Darius, Tone took the opportunity to open the garage and escape the scene before the cops got there. He could've grabbed the gun with his good hand and blasted OG Jesse in the back of his head.

OG Jesse's first thought was to run before the cops and the ambulance got there, but he couldn't leave Darius like this. *Looks like I have to take this one on the chin.*

* * * * *

Jason was no stranger to gunshots going off at his house because there were many attempts on his father's life for his criminal activities. He knew it was coming from inside the garage, and he remembered seeing Darius go in that direction after asking about their father's whereabouts.

As Jason made his way to the garage door, he saw flashing lights from the police and an ambulance glaring through the window shades. He turned right, and that's when he saw his little brother's body on the floor.

"Darius!" he yelled out, but Darius didn't move.

Slowly, Jason moved toward his little brother's body. His yellow Polo shirt was drenched with blood. His small body lay there looking half-dead. Jason went into shock.

Now Jason's body trembled as if he were stuck there in time. The bum's voice seemed to bring him back to the present at the cemetery.

"I still have nightmares about that day," he said.

"Take your time, take a deep breath," the bum advised.

Twice, Jason inhaled and exhaled slowly.

"There you go. You don't have to continue if you don't want to. I'll just be on my way."

"I'm good. I just had a helluva flashback. Where was I?"

The bum reminded him where he'd left off.

Jason continued his story . . .

"Just hold on, you're going to be okay," OG Jesse whispered to Darius, oblivious that Jason was standing there.

OG Jesse knew that once the cops got there and discovered the dead body and a nine-year-old with a gunshot wound to the chest, he had a lot of explaining to do. They were there within minutes, and just like OG Jesse anticipated, the police automatically drew their weapons when they saw the bloody scene.

He just put his hands in the air. "He tried to rob me in my own house, and he shot my nine-year-old son! Do what you got to do!" He put his wrists out to be cuffed.

Jason watched in silence as his little brother was carted off in an ambulance, and his father was hauled off to jail. The paramedics were able to revive Darius in the emergency room. They made it there in record time. Any longer, and he wouldn't have made it.

Fortunately for Darius, the bullet didn't hit any vital organs. It miraculously went in under his left lung and came out by his spine, missing it by an eighth of an inch. The only physical evidence would be a scar the size of a penny on his chest, and one on his back where the bullet exited. The worst scar would be the one left on his mind whenever he thought about that day.

Ironically, OG Jesse received ten to twenty years for the manslaughter of twenty-three-year-old Jeffrey Wilshire. They wanted to give him twenty-five years to life. OG Jesse told the prosecutor that Jeffrey shot Darius, so they couldn't charge him with murder in the first degree. OG Jesse knew the truth that Tone shot

Darius and not Jeffrey, but he had to get some light at the end of this dark tunnel.

"Anything beats getting twenty-five years to life," OG Jesse said after being sentenced. "I'll be back on the streets in no time. Don't count OG out yet."

ALAH ADAMS

CHAPTER 2

BAISLEY PROJECTS
Queens, New York

Darius and Jason were left in the care of their drug addicted mother, Janice. They didn't really know their mother, because she became a crack addict when Jason was six years old and Darius was only two. She left them for dead to pursue her drug of choice. After the shooting, she tried to step up to the plate, but four years later she died from breast cancer, leaving her two boys to fend for themselves.

Before their mother Janice died, she asked Jason to make her a promise. "You have to promise me that you'll take care of your little brother. You can't let me down! If he ends up in a group home, they're going to split you guys up. You have to be a man now, son."

Jason was only seventeen and he had to take care of his thirteen-year-old little brother, who would have a major growth spurt that next year. At just fourteen, Darius was 6-feet 1-inch tall, and Jason grew to 6-feet 3-inches tall. Because of their height, people thought they were older, which gave them an advantage when they were out on the streets.

It was a lot of responsibility for Jason because he couldn't get any public assistance. If he and Darius were sent to live in a group home, they would possibly split them up. The young boys needed money, not now, but right now. So the two brothers did what they thought they had to do—got in the dope game. Darius and Jason contacted one of their father's connects, and just like that he gave them a thousand dollar package. They had to give him $500, which they knocked off in a day. The connect gave them another thousand pack, and while they were selling it, this debonair white man wearing a suit approached them. He introduced himself as George—a Wall Street type, expensive Armani suit, clean cut, blond hair with blue eyes. You'd never expect him to be a drug dealer.

"What's up, fellows? I see you're out here getting a little money for yourselves. How would you like to make more money than you could imagine?" Those were the first words George said to Jason and Darius.

"First of all, you look like a cop. Second of all, who are you?" Darius was always direct.

"My name is George, and I have the best product on the market. When your customers get a taste of my shit, they'll be lined up for blocks trying to cop from you."

"Okay, so where's this shit you talking about? If you about that life, give us a pack. Other than that, you can kick rocks!" Darius boldly told him.

"I like you, you don't hold no punches. Let's take a ride. I don't keep the shit on me."

George took the brothers to a warehouse on Twelfth Avenue in lower Manhattan that was right by a loading dock, and he gave them a kilo of pure heroin just like he said. This shit was the purest heroin on the market, and they were getting it for dirt cheap. Neither brother knew where the dope was coming from. All they did know was that George had an endless supply of it.

Jason and Darius called up their dad's heavy weight customers and let them know they were open for business. They were buying ounces at a time, and before you knew it they had knocked off the whole kilo in one week and made $250,000. All they had to give George was $100,000. Problem solved, right? Not quite, because they were the new kids on the block with all this pure heroin, and everyone wanted a piece. It didn't take long for the wolves to come out and try to eat their food.

"We're getting major money now, can't get caught slipping. That's why I bought this." Darius pulled out a Glock 9-millimeter handgun.

"We don't need that! Where did you get that from?" Guns frightened Jason ever since Darius got shot in his chest.

"You're bugging! We just made $250,000 in a week. I'm not *ever* going to get caught without my hammer on me! You can sleep if you want to."

George gave them two kilos the next time. They sold both in a week and a half. Then he just jumped out the window and started giving them ten kilos every two weeks! Most times they weren't finished with the previous pack before George would give them another ten. Jason and Darius had so much dope they were giving it away for cheap. This allowed other drug dealers to make more money when they got it from the Jensen brothers. They were making cats rich! Fiends and dealers were coming from all five boroughs, New Jersey, and Connecticut to cop from them.

Jason and Darius opened up a trap house on 109th Street and Guy R Brewer Boulevard in Jamaica Queens. Their new spot was clicking so much they had to open for only eight hours a day, and then shut it down. It was just Darius and Jason, but they needed a team. Things were moving too fast.

"Ready to close up shop?" Jason asked Darius as he was counting cash.

"Yeah, let the fiends know we're locking up."

Jason went out and saw only two customers. "We about to shut it down for the day," he told them. Just as he was about to lock the front door, two men stormed in and pulled their guns out.

"Where's the money?" one of them said to Jason. He was so shocked that he didn't say anything. This shit was surreal, until he smacked Jason with the pistol.

Whack!

"You deaf! Take me to the money!"

Damn that shit hurt! Jason thought, rubbing his head.

"It's in the back. Please don't shoot me!" he said with a barrel pointed to his head.

Jason was walking as if he were on the green mile to his own execution. His thoughts were racing. He didn't want Darius getting shot again, and he was willing to give them the money and the drugs if they left them with their lives.

When the robbers and Jason got to the back where he and Darius kept the money and the drugs, Darius was nowhere to be found. *I know I just left him back here counting money. Where the fuck is he at?* The only furniture in the room was a desk with a money counting machine and a laptop sitting on it. They kept the money and the drugs in the desk drawers. Jason panned the room looking for Darius.

Luckily for him about $30,000 rested on the desk. One of the men quickly took out a brown shopping bag and put the money in it. The other one kept his barrel pointed at Jason's temple. He was able to look at the closet door from his peripheral. Darius was pointing his barrel at the gunman collecting the cash.

Jason's heart pounded. It felt like he was about to have a heart attack. He knew there was a slight chance that he was going to get shot that day. Darius had a clean shot at the gunman collecting the money, but the guy with the gun to Jason's head wasn't in his line of fire. He only needed to move a little to the right and Darius could shoot them both.

"Isn't there supposed to be two of them? Where is your partner?" the guy with his gun to Jason's head asked.

"He went to the store."

"Bullshit!" He smacked Jason again in the head with the butt of his gun. "We been watching the spot for two hours, and nobody left in or out!"

A guardian angel must have been with Jason that day because a dope fiend knocked on the door. Both gunmen turned, which gave Darius the chance to let off rounds. Darius hit the first gunman two times, one in the head and the other in his chest, causing him to slump immediately. Jason dropped to the floor when the second gunman turned, which allowed Darius to pop him twice in his dome.

Pop! Pop!

He dropped to the floor as if someone had just pulled his plug.

"You fucked up now!" Darius stood over them and shot them both twice in the head.

Jason hid behind the desk. When the shots went off, his mind flashed back to the day that Darius was shot. His body froze, paralyzed by fear. When Darius finished killing them, Jason remained in hiding. Seeing that the robbers were dead, Darius walked behind the desk and saw his big brother curled up, wide-eyed and shaking.

"You all right?" Darius asked Jason as he kneeled beside him. "Just breathe in and out . . . There you go." Jason started to relax.

When Jason finally stood up and saw pieces of skull and brain mixed with blood, he threw up. The sight of so much carnage made him sick. From that day on, Jason knew he wasn't about that life.

Darius over-killed them, and he didn't even flinch. Jason expected that from a war veteran, not from a fifteen-year-old kid. Then again, the way and place where they grew up was something like a war-zone. They weren't strangers to gunshots, but to Jason's recollection, this was the first time one of them had to kill. That was the day that he knew his little brother was a stone-cold murderer.

"Jason! Are you okay, man?" Darius never saw his big brother like this before, so he didn't know what to do. "Jason! We have to get out of here before the cops come!"

Jason snapped out of it when Darius mentioned the cops. "Let's go!"

When he thought back to that day, his stomach started churning. It was too much for his nerves to continue to sell dope. He wasn't built for this shit. After that incident, Jason was sure that he wanted out. He didn't want anything to do with selling any drug. He couldn't.

"I'm not selling this shit no more. I'm done. You can do it, but I can't do it anymore. I'm out!" he informed Darius.

"What the fuck you mean, you're out? You're never out. You was born into this shit!" Darius was convinced that he was invincible after he killed those two men.

There was nothing Darius could tell Jason, who was walking away from the dope game, and never looking back. They had made enough money that Jason had stashed $150,000 for himself. That would last until he came up with a better hustle.

"I have no college degree and no skilled trade I can use to make money. I'm not trying to go the route of the family hustle: selling drugs and scheming for a living. All I have is my skills as a DJ. I can try that as my new hustle," he said, certain he would go in another direction to earn a living.

AMERICAN D - BOY

True to his word, Jason bought the best new DJ equipment on the market, and then he made some business cards and gave them out to everyone. He worked hard taking DJ jobs for parties, weddings, Bar mitzvahs, you name it he did it. Jason made a name for himself around NYC as DJ Jay-Roc. It took him some time, but in three years, every kid in the city that listened to Hip Hop, knew who DJ Jay-Roc was.

As fate would have it, he landed a gig at Club Delight, one of the biggest clubs in New York City. On his first night of work he met Jazmine Guillermo aka Jazzy, whom he thought was a nice girl. Eventually, Jazzy became his girl and manager. Jason's life was peaches and cream for a minute. He thought because he vowed to stay on the straight and narrow path, he was exempt from catastrophe. Jason, however, found out that no one was safe from other people's bullshit.

He used to preach to Darius. "You don't won't to end up like Dad in prison for years. Selling drugs and doing any crime isn't worth it. Crime don't pay!"

But Darius had a mind of his own. He became content with living a life of crime. It was something he couldn't explain. Darius was a gangster. He had to be, because by the time Darius was eighteen years old, George was giving him close to 100 kilos a month of the purest heroin on the planet. He always wondered where all this pure dope was coming from. What he later found out was mind-boggling!

That's how Darius quickly made a reputation for himself, and he changed his name to D-Boy, the crime-boss. George had put all the heroin in D-Boy's hands, and he supplied the whole city. Living that life was something that came natural to D-Boy. He put together a strong team of goons that helped him sell more dope in other states. He was distributing dope all around the country.

Jason knew he couldn't control his little brother, so he just let him live his life the way he saw fit. He tried to show D-Boy that living that life would get you nowhere fast, but making fast money was everything to D-Boy. Once he got his first taste of fast money, he was off to the races and nothing could stop him except death or prison.

As time passed, Jason was steadily building a name for himself as DJ Jay-Roc, house DJ at Club Delight, doing big parties all over the city. At the same time, Darius was progressively making a name for himself as D-Boy, mega-crime boss. They agreed to disagree and to always stay close no matter what. All they had was each other, and they held each other down. Although Jason didn't like the way Darius was living, yet he had to respect it. They were as different as night and day, but they were brothers and they still loved each other.

A car engine backfired near the cemetery bringing Jason to the present. Anytime he heard gunshots or anything resembling one, it reminded him of his past.

"Damn, that's some deep shit," the bum said while Jason paused to catch his composure. It still hurt him to think that D-Boy was gone.

"The shit gets deeper."

CHAPTER 3

CLUB DELIGHT
New York City

Despite the thirty-eight degree weather, the line to get into Club Delight was around the block. Men and women dressed in their best threads underneath warm winter coats stood at attention like soldiers. The chill factor caused everyone to stand closer to generate warmth. Nothing was stopping them from entering Club Delight, the hottest club in New York City. The biggest celebrities frequented it. All eyes followed the beautiful caramel colored woman with blonde hair as she made her way to the head of the line. "I'm on DJ Jay-Roc's guest list." Everyone knew her as Jazzy. She gave the bouncer her ID.

The bouncer looked at the ID. "Jazmine Guillermo, what's that, Spanish?"

"That's none of your business," Jazzy said, snatching her ID from his fingers.

"Go ahead and let her in."

When she entered the spacious club, she headed straight to the DJ booth. By this time Jazzy and Jason had been an item for four years. She was doing well as his manager, getting him big gigs and keeping his name out there. She and Jason made money and love, all balled up into one nicely kept relationship.

"Hey Jason." Jazzy hugged and kissed him.

"What's popping, beautiful?" he responded.

"What's popping, baby, is that I have some great news for you! I just got a call from DJ T-1 from Hot 104 FM. He offered you a job spinning records for a new show they came up with, called Hot Spot at two!" Jazzy said.

"Wow! Are you serious?" Jason was ecstatic.

"Serious as cancer. He wants you to come in for a meeting."

"Thanks, baby, because I couldn't have done this without the best manager in the world." He hugged and kissed Jazzy passionately.

They were interrupted by Jack, the owner of Club Delight. "Okay, you two lovebirds, you can do that on your own time."

"I'll see you tonight after the club shuts down," he said with a wink.

"Don't be late." Jazzy sashayed away.

Jason went back to doing what he did best, playing the hottest records of the evening.

"Big shout out to DJ T-1 from Hot 104! We about to do big things," he announced in his signature DJ voice.

As he looked out into the crowd, he saw D-Boy with two goons entering the building. They shoved their way through the crowded dance floor to the bar. D-Boy was talking to the bartender, and then he pulled out a massive knot of money to pay for the expensive bottles he ordered. You couldn't help but notice D-

Boy, because he wore three hundred thousand dollars' worth of gold and diamond encrusted jewelry. Everyone watched him in awe as he bought the expensive bottles and proceeded to the DJ booth to greet his big brother, DJ Jay-Roc.

"Here comes trouble," Jack, the club's owner said under his breath. "I thought I told you I didn't want your brother in my club! After that last incident I almost lost my license to operate!"

"I told him that he wasn't allowed on the premises. He doesn't listen to me." *D-Boy doesn't listen to anybody,* Jason thought.

"I'm telling you, Jay-Roc. I'm going to have him—" Jack stopped mid-sentence when he saw D-Boy standing within earshot. "Hey, how you doing, D-Boy?"

"I'm good. What's this my brother's telling me about I can't come into your establishment?" D-Boy always spoke with a signature-scowl on his face. D-Boy glanced at his goons. Their eyes were locked onto Jack like a target.

"No, no, I was just telling your brother that it was a mix-up. We viewed the security cameras, and we saw it was another guy that started the whole thing." Jack spoke fast whenever he was nervous.

"Okay, I was just checking. I wouldn't want anything to happen to this beautiful place by accident. You know what I'm saying?" D-Boy's eyes canvassed the room.

"I agree with you wholeheartedly, D-Boy. Okay, I'm going to let you guys go. I'll have a bottle of

Belaire Rosé Champagne sent up on me." Jack departed before D-Boy could blink.

"I heard what he was saying before he saw me standing there. He's lucky I don't extort his fat ass," D-Boy spoke while popping a bottle of D'ussé.

"I told you not to fuck around with my place of business, Darius! You can do all the bullshit you want out there in the streets, but don't come in here messing up what I got going on!" Jason said sternly.

"Calm down! What I tell you about calling me by my government name? I don't call you Jason while you're at work. I call you DJ Jay-Roc. I'm always at work, so D-Boy is the name! Like I said, you're the only reason I don't lean on his ass and extort him. But anyway, I heard you shouting out DJ T-1 from Hot 104. What's that about?" D-Boy was curious.

"Oh, I got good news. I just got offered a gig at Hot 104 from DJ T-1."

"Say word! Big brother is doing BIG things!" D-Boy took a swig of D'useé from the bottle and tried to pass it to Jason. "Let's celebrate!"

"You know I don't drink. Besides, I have work to do." Jason paused. "Oh yeah, stop by my house tomorrow for an early Christmas dinner. Grandpa Joe is coming through, and Jazzy is cooking one of her Dominican specialties."

"Grandpa Joe is my nigga! I'll definitely be there. I have to talk to him anyway." D-Boy was always excited to see Grandpa Joe. He was the patriarch of the family.

"I'll see you tomorrow. For now I'm going downstairs to bag a honey." As D-Boy moved, his goons followed suit.

You would think that getting shot in the chest at nine years old would make D-Boy more like Jason, calm and humble. Nevertheless, it had an adverse effect on D-Boy. It caused him to not give a fuck about anything or anybody. D-Boy was lawless. In his mind he was the Sheriff, and the world was his town.

Jason watched D-Boy from the DJ booth as he was talking to one of the prettiest girls in the club. Jason smiled before shouting on the microphone, "A big shout out to Don D-Boy in the building!"

D-Boy held up the bottle of D'ussé in acknowledgment.

* * * * *

Two guys from the Haitian Mafia sitting in VIP were watching D-Boy's every move. They were part of a rival drug crew that wanted D-Boy dead. D-Boy took over drug turf in NYC as if it was candy in the palm of a child. George had the best heroin for the cheapest price. There was no way to compete, unless you were growing the shit yourself. They were no match for D-Boy's tactics, but tonight they had strict orders to take him out.

"Let's go," D-Boy said to his goons.

The pretty woman, whose name was Stephanie, walked by D-Boy's side holding on to his arm. They all walked to the valet, and in minutes D-Boy's pearl white CLS 63 AMG Mercedes Benz pulled up in front of the club. The goons scrunched their big frames into the backseat. Stephanie sat in the front.

ALAH ADAMS

"He just walked out. Catch him in front before he leaves," one of the Haitians known as Amos said on the phone to a man waiting outside in a green minivan.

"I'm on it. I see his Benz just pull up in front. As soon as he pulls off, we're going to light his ass up!" the man in the van replied.

When the Benz drove off, they stopped at a light. That's when the green minivan pulled up, and the door slid open. Two men jumped out with automatic weapons. One covered the driver's side, and the other gunman stood on the passenger side with his automatic weapon aimed at the car's windows.

"Oh my god!" Stephanie screamed out. "Just let me out! Please!" She struggled to open the door to no avail. It was locked.

There was a car in front and in back of D-Boy's car, so he couldn't escape. They all looked at the gunmen on both sides before they opened fire with a staccato of bullets. They sprayed the car as if they were holding paint guns. They shot every part of the car with bullets, ensuring that D-Boy was hit multiple times. They shot the car until they both emptied 100 rounds.

"Are you done yet?" D-Boy yelled from inside the car. Before they could answer, two small rectangular shapes opened up on both sides of the car and gun barrels came out. In three seconds, eight shots gunned the two men down right where they stood. "Amateurs! Better luck next time!" The light turned green, and D-Boy left the men drowning in their own blood.

"Good thing I just had this car double bulletproofed. It cost me a small fortune, but it was definitely worth it," D-Boy said as if it were no big deal.

"Good thing you had built-in automatic guns too. That's some next level shit. Never would've gave that a thought, but I'm grateful I didn't get a body full of holes tonight," one of his goons offered.

"You can say that again," the other goon said as he felt his body to make sure the car was indeed completely bulletproof.

Stephanie held her chest with one hand while taking deep breaths. "Please just take me home."

D-Boy smiled.

They drove off unscathed.

The next day, D-Boy pulled up to Jason's apartment in Long Island like nothing happened. He entered the apartment accompanied by the gorgeous woman he met last night, holding a big bottle of Bellaire Rose Champagne. "Hey, what's up, Grandpa Joe!"

"D-Boy, my nigga, even if you don't get no bigger!" Grandpa Joe did a little two-step as he spoke. "Let me hold some money, before you give it to the honeys!"

"Here you go, Grandpa Joe. I always got something for an old school player like yourself." D-Boy pulled out about $15,000 in cash and peeled off $2,500 for Grandpa Joe. "Merry Christmas."

"Thank you, grandson! You always take care of me. I love you to death, D-Boy!" Grandpa Joe was almost in tears.

"Everyone, this is the lovely Stephanie," D-Boy announced.

"Hi, nice to meet you." Stephanie waved at everyone.

"How you doing?" As Jason spoke, Jazzy rolled her eyes.

Stephanie was one of the most beautiful women Jason had ever seen in his life. Brazilian and Asian with green eyes, her high cheek bones glamorized her angelic face. Her smooth, light-brown skin looked kissed by the sun. Stephanie was voluptuous with a small waist. Put it this way: she was the fucking bomb!

Jason winked at D-Boy. "Good choice, little bro," he whispered so Jazzy, who was insanely jealous, wouldn't hear.

"No doubt." D-Boy winked back with a devilish grin.

"Yo, I heard what happened last night when you left the club. Are you okay?" Jason was the first person to find out the news that there was yet another attempt on D-Boy's life.

"Just another day in the life of a gangster. These niggas can't fuck with me!" D-Boy was forever bragging.

You have to understand, D-Boy made the fourth generation of hustlers in the Jensen family. His father OG Jesse Jensen, Grandpa Joe, and Grandpa Joe's father were all certified hustlers. Jason was the only Jensen family member who wasn't involved with anything illegal. He was as straight as an arrow.

"Be careful out there, because it'll be the one closest to you that will take you down. Don't ever sleep on these motherfuckers, D-Boy!" Grandpa Joe spoke with passion.

"I don't sleep, Grandpa Joe. I'll save that for death. It'll be plenty of time to sleep when you die. For now, I'll take short naps, never caught sleeping. You feel me?" D-Boy wasn't lying. He didn't sleep.

Grandpa Joe nodded his approval. "I'm going to tell you a true story of how hustling is in your blood, D-Boy, and that's the real reason it comes so natural to you." Grandpa Joe took a deep breath. He had all eyes and ears.

Ulysses H. Jensen prided himself as a devoted Christian that was holier than thou. Ulysses grew a reputation for being one of the most virtuous slave owners in the south. He was one of the most merciful slave masters, and he did follow the tenants of Christianity, all except one. Ulysses had a secret fetish for his female slaves. Because of his status, his encounters had to be done with the utmost discretion. It was said that our great-great-great grandfather, Stanley Jensen, devised a way to capitalize from the slave master's sexual trysts.

One day after a hard day's work in the cotton field, Stanley requested permission to speak to the owner of the Jensen Plantation, Ulysses H. Jensen himself.

'What business do you have to speak to Master Jensen about?' the overseer asked with a devilish look on his face.

'Well, I just want to give Master Jensen this little wood carving of an eagle that I made for him, in his honor—for his graciousness,' Stanley told the overseer.

41

The overseer snatched the wood carving violently from Stanley's hands and held it up in the air as if inspecting it for authenticity.

After viewing it he spoke, 'All right, Stanley, I'll let you go inside to speak to Master Jensen, but you got two shakes of a bird's feather to get in and out, or you're going to be in a whole heap of trouble! I'm going to whip your black ass till it's raw! You hear me, boy?'

'Yes sir.'

'Now get!'

Stanley quickly entered the big house and was directed to the Master's study where Ulysses was reading a book, the Bible.

'What can I do for you today?' Ulysses asked in the kindest tone Stanley said he'd ever heard come from a white man.

He was hesitant to try his plan because if Ulysses rejected his proposal, it would mean certain punishment from the overseer.

'Well? Speak up,' Ulysses said.

'I . . . well, I know that you like to come out and visit the women down in the slave quarters from time to time. And I know how difficult it is to keep it a secret, especially when you want to see different ones. What's the sense of just having one when you can have as many as you want without the hassle of setting it up yourself?'

Ulysses thought, It is a hassle to set these midnight meetings up on my own without tripping some suspicion.

'What I want to offer you is a service.' Stanley smiled.

'What is this service you speak of?' Ulysses was intrigued by the way Stanley was presenting his business proposal.

'I will set up the time and the secret location for you. I will also have a different girl there for you every time unless you have a craving for a certain one.'

'Okay, what do you want for this service?'

'I want the big slave quarters by the big house, and no more work in the field. I will work the stable because I like horses. And two whole chickens and two slabs of bacon every week.'

Ulysses really needed Stanley's services, but he didn't want to pay him the full amount for them.

'I tell you what, Stanley. I'll give you one whole chicken and one slab of bacon a week, 'cause I still have to give something to the girl. And you can have the big slave quarters.'

'What about no working in the cotton fields and letting me work the stable?' Stanley preferred no work in the field over everything.

Ulysses had to think about that one for a second. What will be my excuse for taking Stanley out of the cotton field and into the stable? Oh I got it! I'll just say that he's a better horse handler than Jasper.

'Okay, Stanley, you got yourself a deal. You can start your new chores in the barn starting tomorrow, and you can move your belongings into the big slave quarters this weekend. And the chicken and bacon can be picked up at the butcher on every Saturday.'

ALAH ADAMS

Stanley acted as if he was thinking about Ulysses' offer, when in fact he was really thinking, Got 'im!

'*Okay, Master Jensen, but after a while, maybe you can throw me that extra chicken and bacon if I does you a good job?*'

Grandpa Joe smiled and nodded his old head full of gray hair. "And that, my son, is the legacy of our family's hustling skills. We've been hustling since slavery, and it don't stop!"

D-Boy loved that story. "That shit is deep, Grandpa Joe! See, my nigga, I knew hustling was in my blood. Now I can prove it! I was born to do this shit! Why you think I'm balling so hard!"

Jason hated that story. "That shit isn't in my blood! I was born to change the game. I'm not trying to end up like Dad, in prison for all those years. You can keep that shit!"

"That's just the way it is. I didn't make the rules. America was built on the hustle. How do you think America got so rich, so fast? A couple of hundred years of free labor, that's how! They mastered the art of hustling motherfuckers!" Grandpa Joe said with passion.

"To each his own. You're right, Grandpa Joe. My job is being a DJ, but I still have to hustle to get more gigs, or I won't eat," Jason added.

"That's right! It's all about the hustle, grandsons, and don't you ever forget it!"

"What's good with that spot at Hot 104?" D-Boy asked Jason.

"Speaking of Hot 104, don't we have that interview tomorrow, Jazzy?" Jason asked.

"Yes sir, we do. I told you that all week. Get it together, brother, get it together," Jazzy replied sarcastically.

"Oh shit! Don't I have to mix in front of them or something?" Jason was already nervous.

"No, it's just like an interview," Jazzy answered.

"I'm about to get up out of here," D-Boy said. Stephanie put her coat on and stood next to him. "Oh yeah, Dad said what's up. I went up to Attica to visit him yesterday. He might be home this summer if he makes his parole board," D-Boy announced while he was gathering his things, getting ready to leave.

"That's what's up! Tell him to call me," Jason replied.

"I will. Good to see you, Grandpa Joe. Call me if you need anything," D-Boy said.

"I definitely will. I love you, D-Boy. Remember what I told you. It's all about the hustle, baby!" Grandpa Joe hugged D-Boy.

"No doubt. I love you too, Grandpa Joe." D-Boy hugged Grandpa Joe tight before letting go.

"Nice meeting you," Stephanie said to everyone.

Ten minutes later, D-Boy and Stephanie got into the Mercedes and drove off. An unmarked FBI vehicle followed. They'd been following him for weeks, trying to catch him slipping. His name came up in a few homicides and in a stash house raid in which they found thirty kilos of heroin and ten handguns. They couldn't pin any of it on D-Boy, but their sources said that he runs the NYC dope game.

D-Boy made a sharp left turn and looked in his rearview mirror to make sure they were still following him. Seconds later, they were making the same turn just like he anticipated. "Keep on coming. I need you to follow me all day, baby."

"Who are you talking to?" Stephanie asked.

"The Feds, they're following me. They think I'm stupid, but I'm always seven steps ahead of them."

D-Boy knew they had been following him for weeks, and he needed them to because it took the attention off his workers that were really getting dirty. D-Boy was no dummy. He knew he couldn't go on for long playing this game of cat and mouse with the FBI. Eventually he was going to lose and he knew it. It was only a matter of time before they came with an indictment with his name written all over it.

"I have to get out of the game before it's too late. Something has to give. I know I can't do this much longer. Shit, they even took down my idol, John Gotti, and I'm nobody compared to him. My brother is right. I have to switch the hustle," D-Boy said.

"I feel you on that one, baby," Stephanie replied.

As he drove, they followed. After taking them on a joyride for an hour, D-Boy got a call from George. "I'm getting an enormous shipment in a couple of days. I should be getting the call from my partner any day. I'm going to need you to step up your game for this one. Think you can handle it?" George asked, knowing D-Boy's answer.

"What's that, a trick question? Of course I can handle it."

"That's my boy. I'm going to be giving you five to ten more kilos in every pack. I'll call you when it gets here." George hung up.

Stephanie gazed at D-Boy, contemplating if she should speak. She went with her gut and decided to speak the truth. "I wish you would give it all up tomorrow . . . everything. The selling, the violence, I want you to live to raise our kids one day." Stephanie spoke from the heart, remembering how open D-Boy had been with her about his upbringing. As they stayed up the previous evening talking, she had come to realize that he was another product of his environment. She wanted to present him with better options for his life because she knew that beneath the thuggery, D-Boy was genuinely a good person.

"Whoa! You going too fast talking about kids," D-Boy replied.

"I'm not saying I want kids from you right now, crazy boy! But you don't want to settle down and have kids one day?"

"Yes, I've thought about it, but not no time soon. Why? Are you trying to have babies now?" D-Boy's tone got serious.

"In the next year or two, yes. And I want a strong man with morals and a good heart to be my children's father. A man like you." Stephanie looked him in his eyes.

D-Boy was caught off guard. "Wow! No woman has ever said that to me before.

"Don't let it go to your head, but yes, I like you a lot," Stephanie admitted reluctantly.

"I happen to like you a lot too."

Stephanie grabbed his hand and kissed it.

Maybe I shouldn't have had that conversation in front of Stephanie. And now she's talking about kids . .

. I'm not trying to have any kids with this broad. I don't even know her like that. I mean, she's beautiful and everything, but she's moving too fast, D-Boy thought. *Wonder what she really wants from me . . . they always want something . . .*

CHAM KALAI VILLAGE
Afghanistan's Eastern Nangarhar province

"We had one of the best poppy growing seasons in history last year. This year we've doubled our production. We are supplying the world with more than 80% of its opiates," Khan said to Captain Jarred Peterson of the United States Army.

"That's what I'm here to speak with you about. There is a demand for more. We need you to produce more because we're running out of the stuff too fast. Especially up in New York, our agent is moving 100 kilos a month through one dealer. He's the richest dope dealer on the east coast," Captain Peterson replied.

"I see. Well, I can produce more, but you have to use your men to secure the western bank of Nangarhar province. Those Taliban fuckers control that land," Khan stated.

"Don't worry about that. I'll have my soldiers go in there and clear them off the land so you can step up the production. Consider it done."

"I'm curious, where is all the stuff going? I mean, I'm already producing over two tons a year. That's enough to get the whole America high." Khan knew he was out of place by asking Captain Peterson this line of questions.

"I'll tell you a little story. Back in Vietnam, in the 60s we controlled the poppy fields. Vietnam used to produce 90% of the world's opiates. We flooded the streets with pure heroin, but things got messy in America. There were junkies all over the place devaluing society. So this go around we got smarter and put the opiates in pills. There are more drug stores per square mile than anything in America. There's millions of prescription pills with your pure opiates in them. Now it's not as messy because the clientele is different. Working class people that are well to do take all the different prescription medications with your powerful substance infused into it." Captain Peterson felt privileged to tell Khan that bit of history.

"I see. That's what makes America much different than the Middle East. We don't use the stuff for recreation because we understand that it can poison the society. It is forbidden. This is the only crop that feeds my family. If there was another crop that made me the same money, I'd gladly stop producing poppy. I hate what it does to people, but your government seems to want to destroy the population with this wicked drug. That's where we differ."

Captain Peterson frowned on Khan for his self-righteousness. "But yet you still grow it, so we're all in this together, Khan. I can easily have my men come and clear you off this land and get another one of you sand-niggers to do the job! Keep your piousness to yourself, are we clear?"

"By all means, we're very clear. I meant no offense. Pardon me if I was misunderstood." Khan faked his apology for fear of being killed.

"My men will be here tomorrow to pick up that quarter of a ton headed for New York." Captain Peterson left the shanty house they were meeting in and made a call.

"Two days and the mother lode will be there," Captain Peterson said.

"That's a little earlier than I expected, but the earlier the better," George replied.

"Your boy is making us a lot of money. He's already made us both multi-millionaires. Before we take him out I want at least $50 million. No loose ends, all we need is some whistleblower to stumble across our operation and we're both fucked." Captain Peterson knew he was talking on a secure line.

"My boy is the biggest dope dealer in New York City and possibly the whole East Coast. I got him. You just keep the shit coming, and we'll both cash out with $50 million," George replied.

"Copy. I'll call you when the bird lands." Captain Peterson hung up and got into the army issued Humvee and drove back to the base.

* * * * *

George sat in the back of a Maybach Benz being chauffeured while in thought about everything he was involved with. *Things are getting deeper than I anticipated. I have to move very carefully, or this whole thing could explode right in my face!*

George, whose real name was Greg Hummel, was a Special Agent working for the Central Intelligence Agency. He was in charge of a covert operation named: BIRDSNEST. Its objective was to take over the poppy fields in the Middle East and use the

50

proceeds from the heroin trade to fund the agency and to line the pockets of the politicians, elite operatives, and high ranking army officers. The Agency had no knowledge of the extra activities he was conducting with D-Boy. If the agency were to find out, he and Captain Peterson would be arrested or even worse. Exterminated!

It was the idea of Special Agent Hummel aka George, to recruit a dealer for his own monetary gain. When he witnessed the amount of cash the Agency was raking in from operation BIRDSNEST, he figured it was time for him to get in the game. He and Captain Peterson were in boot camp together when they were younger, and they stayed in touch and became good friends. George was already recruiting street dealers from the inner cities of America to move product for the Agency, when he stumbled upon Jason and D-Boy. He watched them for weeks before approaching them. He did some research, so he knew about the incident with their father, and then their mother passing. That's when he decided to use them.

In a bizarre way, he thought he was doing the abandoned duo a favor, but in essence he was destroying their lives. What he did do, was create a monster that he knew he'd eventually have to take down. As much as George came to like D-Boy, he knew the day would come when he'd have to murder him. He and Captain Peterson agreed that after they were satisfied with the money, D-Boy had to be taken out.

He took a sip of brandy from a silver flask while reflecting on what had to be done. At the end of the day it didn't matter to him that D-Boy had to go. He knew there would be other dealers from the many ghettos across America that would take his place. The only thing he cared about was saving his own ass.

"Here's to you, D-Boy," he said while taking a healthy swig of the brandy.

CHAPTER 4

INTERVIEW

"**N**ow, this is where shit got crazy," Jason said to the stranger.

"Man, this shit is already crazy," the bum replied.

"The next level is insane though . . . Damn, you have to pardon my manners. What's your name?" Jason asked.

"Oh shit, I got so lost in your story that I forgot to introduce myself. My name is Samuel Miller, but my friends call me Sam."

"You have to pay close attention because things got so twisted I had to convince myself that it was reality. Sam, I can't make this stuff up. Everything I'm telling you is a true story." He took a deep breath to clear his mind . . .

It was Jason's first interview with Hot 104 and the city was having the worst blizzard of the season! Only five days until the New Year and Jason was thinking: new year, new job, this was his big break. It was actually a wake-up call, but he didn't know it yet . . .

"This is it. Remember, let me do the talking," Jazzy said, before entering the Hot 104 conference room.

"You got it, baby. You lead and I follow," Jason responded.

Jazzy and Jason entered the conference room where three people were sitting. They all stood in unison, but only one spoke. "I'm Thomas Weiss. I'm the General Manager of Hot 104. To my left is our Program Director, Tracy Spencer, and of course you know DJ T-1."

"What's up, G?" DJ T-1 said while shaking Jason's hand, then he kissed Jazzy's hand.

Jazzy took that time to give a formal handshake to Tracy and took a seat. Off the top, Jason knew Jazzy didn't like this chick. She didn't get along with females that well for some reason, that's why she didn't have any friends.

"As DJ T-1 discussed with Ms. Guillermo, we are starting a new show called Hot Spot at Two where we will showcase hot new artist. That being said, we want a hot new DJ to host it and that's where DJ Jay-Roc comes in.

"You have an extensive and an impressive resume to be only twenty-five years old. It says here that you started getting paid as a DJ at seventeen years old. In a year, you became the hottest mix-tape DJ in New York City, with a social media network of over 700,000 followers. You've been the house DJ at Club Delight, one of New York City's biggest clubs since you were nineteen, before you could even drink you were rocking parties!" Thomas spoke with enthusiasm.

"Thank you for the props. It's not every day a high level exec respects what I do," Jason said.

Jazzy rolled her eyes. *I told this nigga not to say anything,* she thought.

"Yes, well, like I stated in his bio, he has also won *XXL* Magazine's Mix-Tape DJ of the Year five years in a row. He's not only respected in the U.S., but also overseas in seven countries. He was named hottest up and coming DJ." Jazzy had a habit of speaking arrogantly to people.

"Yes, we see all of his accolades, that's the reason we chose DJ Jay-Roc." Tracy spoke as if she was offended by Jazzy's demeanor.

Noticing the catty display brewing between the women, Thomas intervened. "Let's get down to business, shall we?" He went into a folder and started reading. "Your first payment is for $75,000 for the first quarter. If your show fails to bring in high ratings in the first quarter, we will dismiss the show entirely. However, if your show is able to get high ratings, then your pay for the second quarter will be $80,000. You'll receive a $5,000 bonus every quarter you receive high ratings."

"Do you have this in writing?" Jazzy asked, pretending to be professional.

Thomas held up a stack of four pages stapled together in one hand. "It's all made out simple in this contract, and this piece of paper." Thomas held up a check that read SEVENTY-FIVE THOUSAND DOLLARS in his other hand.

Shocked by the digits on the check, Jason almost lost his composure. He didn't want to seem hungry for the money, so he kept his cool and shook his head. *It's been a while since I paid my bills on time,* he thought.

He looked at the check and then he looked at Jazzy. She just shrugged. It was Jason's call.

"Sign it," she said through clenched teeth.

Jason signed the deal, and that fast they had a check for seventy-five thousand dollars.

"Welcome to the Hot 104 family, DJ Jay-Roc." Tracy gave him a tight hug and a kiss on the cheek that didn't miss Jazzy's attention.

Jazzy would've responded in true ghetto fashion, but something else was going on at the same time that required her attention. She was reading a text message from DJ T-1 who was sitting right in front of her.

DJ T-1: *When you get a chance call me. But you need to be alone, I don't want to sound fishy, but you'll understand when I tell you what I have to say. It's an opportunity to make some serious side money under the table. Double the check they just gave you in the first month. I'll call you at 8 p.m. sharp.*

Jazzy: Ok. 8 sharp.

"Congratulations, DJ Jay-Roc! Your show will start on January 2, right after the New Year," Thomas said before exiting the meeting.

Jazzy and Jason were quiet until they were downstairs and outside walking down the street. They were both ecstatic about what just happened. They'd put in a lot of work to get here. This was one of Jason's ultimate goals, to be a DJ on a reputable radio station. So for him, this was a dream come true.

AMERICAN D - BOY

"I can't stand that bitch, Tracy! I saw her kiss you on the cheek. I should've smacked her in her damn face," Jazzy spoke in her signature *mean girl* tone.

"That was harmless. She was just welcoming us to the family," Jason said in Tracy's defense.

"Fuck her. Let's go cash that check! We have to celebrate tonight!"

"No question, I might even take a sip of some champagne tonight," he said to her surprise.

"I have to go freshen up, so I'll meet you at Club Delight at say like 9:30." She had to make herself available at 8 p.m. to talk to DJ T-1.

"Sounds like a plan. I'm going to deposit this check." He hugged and kissed Jazzy, and they parted ways.

* * * * *

DJ T-1 was right on schedule. He called at eight on the dot. "Hello, DJ T-1?"

"What up, Jazzy?" he asked nervously.

"I don't know, you tell me."

"Let me cut to the chase. There are hundreds of artist trying to get their music heard on a major radio station like Hot 104. I have a list of about eighty artist that are willing to pay thousands of dollars to achieve that goal. This new show gives DJ Jay-Roc the ability to add songs to the playlist without going through the Program Director. He is responsible for finding the new artist that will air on the Hot Spot at Two. Normally it's the Program Director that compiles and approves the songs on the playlist. So what I want you to do is give him the songs that should be played on the Hot Spot at Two. I'm asking for $10,000 to play

57

one song on the radio for a few spins. I'll split it with you 50/50." DJ T-1 paused.

"I don't get it. You're telling me that we can collect $10,000 for playing one song? Does the station have to know about it?" Jazzy asked.

"That's the only thing. It's illegal to take money to play records, and it's a Federal offense. It's called *Payola* and it's punishable by jail time and heavy fines. That's why everything must be done with the utmost discretion."

"So who gets in trouble in the event we're caught?" She knew the answer to her own question.

"The DJ who played the records." There was an awkward silence.

"You have to let me think about this because I'm not trying to get my boyfriend put into prison for playing records on a radio station."

"Hold up. DJ Jay-Roc is your boyfriend? How can you manage your boyfriend?"

"It's a long story, but I don't know if I can do this. You'll have to let me think on it for a few days."

"Okay, but you know what they say: study long, study wrong." DJ T-1 hung up the phone without warning.

Jason grew silent for a moment. The sound of an ambulance reminded him that he was at the cemetery talking with a complete stranger.

"Wow! The way it sounds, I bet she started taking the money," Sam said.

"She did more than that, and DJ T-1 wasn't who he appeared to be." Once again, Jason didn't want to jump ahead of the story. "In order for you to understand, I can't skip through it, because there's more to all this shit than meets the eye. Trust me."

Sam moved closer to Jason, fully prepared to take it all in.

ALAH ADAMS

CHAPTER 5

JASON'S APARTMENT
Long Island, New York

On New Year's Eve, Jazzy and Jason were at his apartment splitting up the cash. It was one of the happiest moments of his life. Jazzy was happy, but she showed him a different side. Jason should've known from that day, that Jazzy was money hungry. But you know what they say: "Love is blind."

"I can't believe it took five days for the check to clear," Jazzy said in dismay.

"I know, good thing it cleared today. Can you believe we got $75,000 cash on New Year's Eve?" He divided the money into two piles. One pile was significantly bigger than the other. Jason closed his eyes whenever he was doing math in his head. "Let's see, 20% of $75,000 is $15,000." Jason slid the smaller pile of money toward Jazzy. "Here you go, baby."

Jazzy looked at the small pile of money as if it were bacteria. She didn't touch it, but she just glared at it in disgust.

"Earth to Jazzy! Baby, are you all right? You had me worried there for a second. I thought you were about to pass out or something. You were just staring into outer space, in a trance."

"I'm okay. I was just thinking about what I was going to do with all this money."

"Let's go shopping so we can be extra fresh for the Hot 104 New Year's Eve party tonight." Jason couldn't contain his excitement.

Jazzy and Jason went all out for the Hot 104 New Year's Eve party. They rented a limo and were dressed like celebrities, wearing the latest designer fashion. The two looked like new money, because they were *new money*.

When they arrived they were ushered to the V.I.P. to be with the rest of the Hot 104 family. Jason saw DJ T-1 and they made eye contact, and then he looked at Jazzy.

"What's up, DJ T-1? I want to thank you again for putting me on at Hot 104. This is like a dream come true for me," he humbly said to DJ T-1 as he approached them.

"Don't mention it. We needed some new talent at the station anyway." DJ T-1 looked at Jazzy. "How're you doing, Jazzy?"

"I'm good." Jazzy seemed distracted as she sent a text to someone.

"Who're you texting, baby?" Jason asked.

"Oh, that was my home girl Tasha wishing me a happy New Year. Let's hit the dance floor."

While Jason and Jazzy were on the dance floor he spotted D-Boy. Something was different about him. He wasn't with his goons. D-Boy was with Stephanie and he looked happy. When D-Boy spotted Jazzy and Jason, he strolled over with Stephanie in tow.

"You remember my big brother, DJ Jay-Roc," D-Boy said to Stephanie with a smile, which was rare. "And Jazzy." He stopped smiling when he said Jazzy's name.

"Of course I remember your brother, silly." Stephanie smiled. "Hi Jazzy, you look stunning in that dress."

"Thank you, you don't look too bad yourself." Jazzy was in rare form—she didn't like to give compliments.

Jazzy and Stephanie were talking, so D-Boy and Jason had a little sidebar of their own.

"Jay, I think I'm feeling shorty. She makes my day. I've never felt like this about a woman." D-Boy smiled.

"That's what's up. I'm happy for you, little brother."

While Jason was talking with D-Boy, DJ T-1 approached Jazzy. "Can I have this dance?"

"Sure," she replied. "Baby, I'm going to dance with DJ T-1 if you don't mind."

"Of course not," he replied.

DJ T-1 and Jazzy disappeared into the sea of dancing celebrators. Jason dipped off to the car, glancing back with suspicion.

* * * * *

DJ T-1 danced close enough to talk in her ear without notice. "You made the right decision. What made you change your mind?"

"When I got my 20%, which was only $15,000 out of $75,000. That's when I said fuck it, I'm down."

"I figured you would see the dollar signs."

As they danced, DJ T-1's penis became erect. Jazzy didn't pull back, so he dry humped her backside. They were so caught up in the moment they didn't notice D-Boy watching them.

I knew that bitch was a sneaky no good ho! Wait till I tell my brother! D-Boy thought. *I bet my brother wouldn't like this shit.*

Then something strange happened. D-Boy caught eye contact with DJ T-1. *I don't know what it is, but I know DJ T-1 from somewhere. I just can't put my finger on it. It's something about this dude I don't like.* D-Boy was stuck in his thoughts until Stephanie grabbed his manhood and distracted him.

"I'm feeling hot, daddy," she whispered in his ear.

D-Boy looked around for Jason. "Where is this nigga at?"

He continued to search for him until he saw him returning with a full length black mink in his hands.

"I know this fool ain't about to give this slut that mink!" D-Boy murmured as he looked down at his Rolex. It was almost count down to the New Year.

Jazzy was done dirty dancing with DJ T-1. She quickly strolled over to Jason. "Hey baby, what's that in your hand?" She knew exactly what it was. "Whose mink is that?"

"Ten, nine, eight, seven, six, five, four, three, two, one—HAPPY NEW YEAR!" everyone screamed in unison.

"It's yours." Jason slipped the expensive coat onto her shoulders, while reaching into its pocket. "Baby, you've been my light in the darkness, my love, you're my everything. For all that you are, Jazmine Guillermo, will you marry me?" Jason pulled out a three carat princess cut diamond ring with baguette diamonds all around the sides.

"It's beautiful, Jason!" Her eyes began to well up with tears.

"Well, will you?" he asked, nervous.

"Yes, of course I will marry you, Jason Jensen!" Jazzy hugged him with all her might before kissing him.

D-Boy was walking up when he saw his brother pull the ring out. He couldn't hear the words, but it looked exactly like a proposal to D-Boy.

"I hope this fool isn't proposing to this skank," D-Boy grumbled as he stood within arm's reach and saw Jason place the ring on her finger. "Damn, I'm too late!" He watched Jazzy and Jason hugged in a lover's embrace and witnessed how happy his big brother was, as if he was glowing from bliss. He'd never seen Jason this happy in all his life. *I'm not going to spoil it for you tonight, big bro. I see you all happy and shit. I'm going to be watching Jazzy and that DJ T-1. I know what I saw. Those two are up to something. And if I find out Jazzy is doing my brother wrong, her and DJ T-1 will be sleeping with the fish. For now enjoy yourself.*

D-Boy raised his glass in the air in a toast while staring directly at DJ T-1, and then at Jason and Jazzy.

Happy fucking New Year!

AMERICAN D-BOY

While D-Boy's attention was focused on Jazzy and Jason, Stephanie got a call. She used to have a soft spot for Agent Anthony Trenton. He was tall and muscular, with the facial structure of Brad Pitt. In fact, he often got compliments for favoring the famous actor. What she didn't like was his arrogance. Trenton came from a privileged background, so he habitually degraded minorities without realizing Stephanie was one of them.

"Happy New Year, Steph. I really miss you. Can we talk?" Agent Trenton asked.

"Not right now," she replied to her ex-lover.

"Why are you so cold towards me lately? I hope you aren't falling for this low-life D-Boy character. You'd be risking your whole career if you made that stupid mistake."

"I have to go. I don't want to go back and forth with you anymore. Goodbye." Stephanie hung up just as D-Boy approached.

"Who was that?" D-Boy asked suspiciously.

"That was my boss wishing me a happy new year." She kissed him on the cheek. "I can't wait to get home so we can have a private celebration."

"Let's go back to my place. I got a cold gold bottle of Ace of Spades we can pop." His cell began ringing and he glanced at the number. "Hold on, baby. Let me take this call." He stepped a few paces away and plugged his left ear with his finger to ward off the club noise.

D-Boy always took calls from his lawyer, John Gillespie. No matter the time of day or night, he knew

John only called when there was important information. D-Boy had one of the most powerful lawyers in the country. He didn't just specialize in the law, he was also an expert in counter intelligence. D-Boy paid John large sums of money, and he didn't have a case. D-Boy paid him to investigate everybody in his circle. Everyone that ever worked for, or had any dealings with D-Boy, were all being watched by private investigators that were dispatched by the Law Firm of Levi, Dunningham, & Swartz.

"D-Boy, the girl Stephanie is a red flag! I repeat, she is a red flag! Don't say anything or do anything around her. She is FBI!" John said frantically.

"Get the fuck out of here! That's impossible. I've been to her job, and she's an accountant." D-Boy didn't want to believe it, but it was true.

"She's deep under cover. They've been placing her in your path, knowing you'd one day go for her. Think about it."

D-Boy thought back to how they first met at Club Delight. He did see her there frequently before he approached her. Stephanie was also a regular at two other spots that D-Boy hung out at, the Cheetah Club and Perfections.

"This can't be!"

"Be very careful," John told him before hanging up.

D-Boy cursed.

"What happened, baby?" Stephanie asked, noticing him getting emotional.

D-Boy ignored her. "I'll take care of it." He hung up.

"Who was that?" Stephanie asked.

"My lawyer. He had some disturbing information for me."

"I'm sorry to hear that. What was it about?"

"One of my workers isn't flying straight. Matter fact, let me make this call. Excuse me." D-Boy made sure he was out of earshot.

"Is everything okay?" Stephanie asked once he returned to her side.

"Of course, you ready to get up out of here?" D-Boy asked.

"I'm ready when you are," she replied.

When they got in the Mercedes and drove off, a black SUV followed them.

D-Boy was quiet during the whole ride to the house. Stephanie noticed, but she remained silent as well. She didn't want to break his train of thought, but she was beginning to worry. Was her cover blown? D-Boy had just gone from hot to cold in an instant.

As the car neared D-Boy's home, Stephanie noticed a van following them. The minute he pulled into the driveway, she glanced to her left, seeing the van now parked a half block down. That's when she knew the van was indeed following them. Her thoughts went into survival mode, and her training as an agent kicked in.

I'm not letting them take me out. She peeped inside her clutch purse that held her compact 32 automatic. *What am I going to do?* Her intuition screamed that D-Boy somehow knew she was an FBI agent. *I have to go with my heart,* she thought.

D-Boy opened his car door to exit.

"Wait! Get back in the car. There is something I have to tell you," Stephanie announced suddenly. The expression on her face told D-Boy what she had to say was serious.

"What is it?" he asked, looking irritated.

She took a deep breath before speaking. "You know that I love you, right?"

"I don't know about that." He turned away from her gaze, staring straight ahead.

"I'm about to prove it to you." She paused. "I'm an agent for the Federal Bureau of Investigations. You are my assignment, but the time I've spent with you has made me feel your pain, and I don't want to do this for them anymore."

D-Boy gripped the steering wheel with all his might and exhaled.

"I'm not turning in any evidence that will get you convicted of any crime, because I'm in love with you, Darius Jensen."

D-Boy was stunned. He wasn't expecting her to reveal herself. Yet he still showed her his hand. "I already know. My lawyer just told me."

"I'm sorry for lying to you in the beginning. I was just doing my job."

"Don't worry about it. I respect that you came clean because you're putting your own freedom on the line."

"I don't care! I've never felt like this about a man in my life." Tears strolled down her face. "Let's just run away, you have enough money. We can start over in another country like Dubai, or Sweden."

"I can't. I have obligations."

"Can I ask you a question? Do you love me?" She searched his face for any signs of proof.

D-Boy looked at her, then he pulled out his cellphone. "Yo, scratch that."

When he hung up the phone the van started up and left the premises.

"I think I do love you."

She knew exactly what that call meant, that she was about to be fish food.

"Let's go inside and have a conversation." D-Boy escorted her inside.

They talked for hours, both laying all their chips on the table. It was a relief for Stephanie because she wanted to be honest with the man she was falling in love with.

They stayed up all night talking and making love until the sun came up. Their future still remained uncertain.

ALAH ADAMS

CHAPTER 6

"I CAN'T FUCK THIS UP!"

He was in love with her. She was the only woman that D-Boy ever loved." Jason paused. "It's getting dark and they're about to shut the cemetery down. Would you like to have dinner? We can finish our conversation over a meal, on me," Jason offered.

"Hell yeah! As you can tell, I'm not doing so well, so I'd appreciate it."

"It's the least I can do. I'm venting and it's therapeutic. There's a Jamaican restaurant called Island Cuisine that I like to eat at. It's around the corner."

"Cool," Sam said.

Jason and his newfound friend walked slowly toward Island Cuisine. When they arrived they were seated and given menus.

"Okay, where was I?"

"You were going to tell me about the radio gig," Sam said.

"Oh, right. That's when chaos nearly destroyed my career," Jason responded, looking out toward the huge window and into the past...

70

Jason was so anxious about his first day at Hot 104. *I can't fuck this up! I've never been this nervous in my whole life. I have to pull it together. Come on, Jay-Roc. Do what you do,* he thought, right before entering the DJ booth to do the first show.

"Are you okay? You're sweating like crazy. Get a hold of yourself," Jazzy said, noticing sweat pouring down his face like a faucet.

DJ T-1 was on the sideline watching, waiting for Jason to disappear so he could conduct business, and possibly some pleasure with Jazzy. He couldn't get that dance out of his mind, and neither could she.

Jazzy found herself daydreaming about the dance when she woke up, then she looked at the ring and remembered the engagement. *Damn, I can't believe I'm engaged.*

"Here goes a towel, my dude," DJ T-1 offered. "I know the feeling. I was the same way the first day of my show. That was almost ten years ago."

"Thanks, man. That just made me feel a lot better. I appreciate that, DJ T-1."

Not as much as I'm going to appreciate tapping your girl's ass, DJ T-1 thought before speaking. "Don't mention it, brother."

Jazzy watched the friendly exchange between DJ T-1 and Jason. She found DJ T-1 to be very strategic.

"Twenty seconds till show time," Tracy announced. "Happy New Year, Jason."

"It's DJ Jay-Roc to you," Jazzy said directly.

Tracy stared at Jazzy as if she were a foreign object. "I'm sorry, umm, what is your name again?"

"My name is Jazzy, the soon to be *Mrs. Jensen.*"
Jazzy held up the three carat ring to Tracy's face, then
wiggled her fingers to reflect the bling off the lights.
"Like I said, you'll be addressing my fiancé as DJ Jay-
Roc."

"No problem, Jazzy." Tracy smiled before heading
to her office. *She needs to get her teeth fixed before
she come in here acting super-fly,* Tracy thought as she
stepped away.

"New York City, Long Island, Upstate, New
Jersey, Connecticut and the whole world! It's your
boy! DJ Jay-Roc!" Jason pressed a button and horns
went off like an alarm. "Many of you know me from
rocking parties at Club Delight, and if you don't know
me, you better ask somebody! I'm your host with the
most, man of the hour, too sweet to be sour! DJ Jay-
Roc is in the building for your listening pleasure! It's
the Hot Spot at Two! Where you'll hear everything
new! Let's get it!"

Jason Jensen was a different person when he was
DJ Jay-Roc. Jason was shy and quiet. DJ Jay-Roc was
loud and outgoing. Jason learned how to turn it on and
off at will. Being DJ Jay-Roc gave him a chance to
express himself in a way that was more therapeutic
than anything. Jason became withdrawn after D-Boy
was shot and his father went to jail, so he used the
turntables to escape. When Jason was DJ Jay-Roc, he
was in a zone.

The second DJ Jay-Roc was on air, DJ T-1 wasted
no time approaching Jazzy. "Excuse me, Jazzy. Can I
speak to you in my office for a moment?"

"Sure."

Jazzy followed DJ T-1 to his office. He closed the door and locked it before they took a seat. "This is music from the first five clients." He slid her a CD along with a list of artists and song titles. "When he plays all of their music, you'll get your money." DJ T-1 was a little cold toward Jazzy because he heard her tell Tracy that she was engaged.

"Is that all?" Jazzy noticed his attitude and didn't care to stroke his ego.

"Actually no, that isn't all I have to say." DJ T-1 stood up. "I can't get you off my mind. I want you so bad I can taste it."

Jazzy had to take a deep breath because DJ T-1 was turning her on, but she didn't want to lead him on. She really loved Jason, and she didn't want to betray him. But there was something about DJ T-1 that allured her to him, and they both knew it without saying it.

Truth be told, Jason wasn't really Jazzy's type. She loved danger and adventure and Jason was the total opposite. Jazzy grew up in a hustling household just like he did. She was the daughter of a Dominican drug lord. Her father was more like D-Boy than DJ Jay-Roc. Jazzy just settled for Jason because she wanted something different. She was used to dealing with men like D-Boy and DJ T-1, but the outcome was always the same—hurt and disappointment. Though she was hurt by these types of men, she was still highly attracted to them.

"Well, you won't be tasting this. I'm sure you heard the news." She held up her ring. "I'm engaged. I'm sorry if you got the wrong impression last night." Jazzy stood. "If you'll excuse me, my fiancé needs my attention." Jazzy exited the office.

When Jazzy was out of DJ T-1's sight, she had to close her eyes and compose herself. *I can't let my emotions get the best of me.*

Jazzy stopped at the vending machine to get a bottled water before making her way down the hall to the room where Jason did his show.

Jason was taking a quick commercial break. "Hey baby, where were you?"

"I had to meet with DJ T-1 about the playlist. He gave me a few hot new artists for us to play on the show. I think these artists will make the show pop!"

"Okay, that's what's up! I'll play them right after the break."

Jazzy watched as Jason was about to unknowingly commit a felony so that she could make more money. The guilt was like a small storm forming in the pit of her stomach. In time it would become a category 5 hurricane.

This is all wrong! Jazzy shouted in her mind. *I have to stop him before he plays any of those songs!*

Just as Jazzy opened the door, Jason was introducing the first artist. "This first artist I'm about to introduce to the world is a cat named Shoota. The song is called, 'I'm the New John Gotti.' He's bringing that gangster ish back to New York. The second artist is a nineteen-year-old prodigy they call Top Notch. He's heating it up with his single 'Shake it Fast.' You heard it here first! It's your boy, DJ Jay-Roc! Let's get it!" He winked at Jazzy when he saw her approach.

AMERICAN D - BOY

She passed him a bottled water and gave him a kiss on the cheek before exiting.

He played all five songs on his show, and he also promoted the artist by talking about them, which did wonders for their careers. People automatically called the station asking questions about all the new artists. All the calls were directing people to buy the music from iTunes, which turned into revenue. So everybody gets paid, the DJ, the station, and the artist.

"That's a wrap! I hope you enjoyed the Hot Spot at Two! I'm your host, DJ Jay-Roc! Peace & Blessings!" Jason exited the booth to be greeted by the whole Hot 104 staff clapping their hands.

"Great show, DJ Jay-Roc!" a short white kid with dreadlocks said, giving him a handshake. He was followed by ten more guys and of course, Tracy.

"Congratulations on a great show, DJ Jay-Roc!" Tracy smiled two perfect pearly white rows of teeth. "Can I have everyone's attention? I want to make an announcement. According to the National Radio Ratings Association, DJ Jay-Roc has just broken a record for the most volume of listeners for a debut radio show!" Everyone applauded except DJ T-1. He ice-grilled Jason instead of giving him praise.

No one knew why DJ T-1 was upset but Tracy. The record that Jason just broke was none other than DJ T-1's himself. Before today, DJ T-1 held the record for the most volume of listeners for the debut of a show. In radio world that's a big deal.

Tracy had a gripe with DJ T-1 because they used to be lovers, until he dumped her for her best friend.

Even though her ex-BFF dumped DJ T-1, Tracy still wanted to use this opportunity to rub his nose in it.

"Sorry, DJ T-1, you used to have that record. Maybe you can try to break another record before you retire." One of the interns chuckled.

"Ha ha, very funny." DJ T-1 didn't take it to heart. He had bigger fish to fry, so he went straight to his office. *I just made $50,000 in two hours. Do you think I give a fuck about DJ Jay-Roc breaking my old record? And I have a whole list of artists ready to pay.*

Out of the five new artists Jason played, the first two, Shoota and Top Notch stood out. They got the most calls, the most requests, and the most iTunes sold in a day. In fact, their songs, "I'm the New John Gotti" and "Shake it Fast" got so many requests, the radio station had to play them three more times that day. DJ T-1 was impressed with their reception so much that he wanted to offer them both a deal.

DJ T-1 dialed Shoota's number. The phone rang three times before Shoota answered. "Yo, the streets are going crazy right now! My single is popping! Good looks, my nigga!" Shoota was so excited he couldn't contain himself.

"That's what I'm calling about. I have a deal for you. The next song you want to get played will only cost you $5,000. The song we played today will be in rotation because of the amount of requests it's getting."

"It's all good, T-1. I just have to run it by my manager. It should be a go though."

"Okay, let your manager know the deal and get back to me ASAP." *Damn, I wanted to be his manager. Oh well, you can't win them all.* DJ T-1 hung up. *Then again maybe I can.*

* * * * *

Shoota couldn't wait to call his new manager to tell him the news. "We did it! I couldn't have done it without you, D. If you wouldn't have put up that money for me, none of this would've happened. I just got a call from DJ T-1 telling me we can get our new songs on the radio for half the price."

"That's what's up! You know I got it! Let's get it."

"I can't even thank you enough, D."

"Don't worry about it, just keep making them hits. I have to go. I have some business to attend to. Call me later," D-Boy said before hanging up. *This music shit might just be my way out of the streets,* he thought as he drove his Mercedes Benz through the streets of New York.

As usual, the FBI was following D-Boy. This time they decided to flash their lights and pull him over. Two FBI agents got out of the vehicle and approached D-Boy slowly with their guns drawn.

"Easy, fellows, you don't have to pull your weapons out," D-Boy said when he saw their weapons drawn.

"Shut the fuck up and get out of the vehicle!" Agent Trenton yelled.

"Okay, you got it. I'm getting out of the car." D-Boy knew this was some extra shit.

Agent Trenton slammed D-Boy against the car. "We know what you do and who you are, you piece of shit!"

77

ALAH ADAMS

"Get your fucking hands off of me! Either charge me with something or let me go!" D-Boy's lawyer taught him his rights.

The agent pressed up against D-Boy. "I'll be watching you, and you might've gotten away with a lot of shit in the past, but you won't dodge the charges I have waiting on you."

"You threatening me, Agent Trenton? My lawyer is so powerful that he'll have you working at the desk for the rest of your career. Fuck with me."

Agent Trenton knew that John Gillespie was very powerful, and he could have his badge. No one in the agency messed with John Gillespie. He had taken down many corrupt officers. Agent Trenton backed up off D-Boy when he thought about messing with John.

"You got this one, D-Boy. But you better watch your back." With that being said, the two agents got back into their car and drove off.

D-Boy saw his reflection in the window of his car. His image wasn't clear for some reason. Even though he wasn't superstitious, he took that as an odd sign, that the blurry reflection represented something much deeper.

That's when D-Boy knew he had to get out of the game.

78

CHAPTER 7

NEW YORK STATE THRUWAY

his Benz drives like a spaceship!"
Shoota said with excitement.
"You keep making dope music and you can buy ten of these," D-Boy responded.

"How often do you take this drive upstate to see your pops?" Shoota asked.

"Like, five times a year. I take him money, clothes, sneakers, and sometimes I bring him drugs so he can sell them in there. You get ten times more money in there for dope."

D-Boy and his father were very close. OG Jesse schooled D-Boy to the ways of the game. D-Boy understood his father—they shared the same lifestyle. Jason on the other hand, talked to OG Jesse on the phone, but today was the first trip he took to visit him in a while. OG wasn't mad, in fact he admired Jason for taking the high road in life.

"That's some G shit, to be cool with your pops like that. I never knew my father. He could be standing right in front of my face and I wouldn't know it."

Shoota always felt some type of way whenever he spoke about his absentee father.

"Sorry to hear that. A man needs a father. My dad was always there. He got locked up when we were young, but we were big kids when that happened," D-Boy said.

"We used to think Dad was an athlete when we were young. Eventually we found out the truth," Jason added.

"Damn, how long does it take to get to Attica? It seems like we've been driving forever," Shoota asked.

"I know, that's why I don't visit him often. It's like an eight hour drive from NYC," Jason said.

Shoota was a cool dude. D-Boy didn't usually make friends, but he and Shoota seemed to have a lot in common. Shoota was from the streets, so he could identify with D-Boy. Jason figured if he was cool with D-Boy, then he was cool with him. Besides, he was backing anything positive that D-Boy did. It's rare for him to do anything besides sell heroin.

"I'm going to take a nap back here. Wake me up when we get to Attica." Jason needed some well-deserved rest.

"Okay," D-Boy replied.

With that being said, he closed his eyes in search of sleep, barely hearing the conversation between Shoota and D-Boy.

"If it wasn't for you I wouldn't have had the money to get my songs played on Hot 104. I'm moving units on iTunes. People want me to perform, and DJ T-1 told me he got me on the next song for half price."

AMERICAN D - BOY

"I'm curious, how does it work? You just give DJ T-1 ten thousand and he plays your songs?" D-Boy was really trying to find out other info.

"I did this showcase and DJ T-1 was there. He heard my music and told me he liked it. We exchanged numbers. One day he called me. He told me he was putting together a new show for the New Year. That's when he told me if I wanted to get my song on the radio I had to pay ten thousand. I asked you for the money and you kept it official. The rest is history."

"Most people don't know that DJ Jay-Roc is my brother. I keep it that way because I have a lot of beef out here in these streets." He kept Jason away from his lifestyle out of respect. To keep him safe from his beef as well.

"I knew who DJ Jay-Roc was, but I didn't know he was your brother. I knew you for a few years now, and I didn't make the connection. Wow, it's a small world!"

Note to self: ask my brother if he's getting any of that ten thousand, D-Boy thought.

They started seeing signs that read: 10 miles to ATTICA. It didn't take long before they were parked and entering the infamous ATTICA CORRECTIONAL FACILITY.

"Wake up, Jay! We're here," D-Boy announced.

"Damn, son, this shit look like a haunted castle or some old spooky shit," Shoota said, when they approached the mammoth structure.

"I know, that's the same shit I said when I first came here." Jason hated coming here.

81

The guards treated everyone the same, as if visitors were prisoners themselves. They were nasty to everyone, even the women and children. They made sure visitors understood where they were, even if they did get to leave. For the six hour visit, family and loved ones were subject to the treatment of an inmate.

"Do they always act like that?" Shoota asked, noticing the guard's attitude toward everyone.

"Yeah, they're Class A dickheads. I'm used to it," D-Boy said.

"That's the other reason I don't come here. I hate the way the guards treat everyone," Jason added.

All three men sat at a table waiting for OG Jesse to appear. It didn't take long before he came strolling in looking like the hulk. OG Jesse was one of the biggest inmates in Attica. He held the record for bench pressing the most weight in the yard. And the record for knocking out the most men in a single year. OG knocked out twenty-six men. No one messed with OG Jesse Jensen!

"What's up, Jason and D-Boy?" Jesse hugged both of his sons with his huge arms. "Who's this motherfucker?" Jesse looked at Shoota as if he was going to kill him. Just when he couldn't take it anymore, he burst out laughing. "I'm just fucking with you, man. What's up, young blood? They call me OG Jesse Jensen," he said while shaking Shoota's hand.

"What's up, OG? You had me bugging for a second. I didn't know what to think." Shoota laughed it off.

"This is my new artist, Shoota. I'm getting into the music business. There's a lot of money to be made," D-Boy said.

OG Jesse was always interested in the term, *a lot of money*. "Tell me more about it."

"You know Jason got a job hosting a show at Hot 104?" D-Boy asked, not sure if Jason told him.

"Yeah, he told me about that. I'm very proud of you, Jason. You may not have turned out like me, D-Boy, and Grandpa Joe, but you're a stand up dude. Somebody has to go the square route."

"Well, after D-Boy was shot, and I was pistol whipped, I knew I wasn't about that life." Jason wasn't ashamed of his decision to get out of the game. He just wanted D-Boy to get out before it's too late.

"I want to get out of the game eventually, that's why I'm investing into the music business. Jason played Shoota's song on the radio for the first time a week ago and the city went crazy! If things go well, I'm getting out the game," D-Boy said.

"Why not get all the money? Get the rap money and the dope money, it's all the same," OG Jesse argued.

"If we make it big in music, we won't need to sell dope anymore. I'm talking about making it big like Jay-Z, half a billion on these bitches!" D-Boy responded.

"When you put it that way, you're right," OG Jesse agreed.

"That's why I fucks with this nigga," Shoota said. "I like that type of talk. We going straight to the top!"

OG was feeling Shoota's energy. He knew his son was on to something. OG sat quietly shaking his head. "You know I go to my second parole board this summer. It's going to be a wrap if they let me go."

"I know, that's why I'm going to have a spot waiting for you in this music business. We're going to make it a family business! You're the muscle, Jason is the DJ, and we have a dope artist." He pointed to Shoota. "And we have money to make it happen."

"Plus I have the highest rated radio show in NYC." Jason chimed in.

"I feel like God put us together to make history! I'm a loyal dude, and I got songs for days! We're going to take over this game!" Shoota was turned up.

"Keep it down! Or we're going to ask you to leave!" one of the guards shouted to Shoota.

"My bad, officer," Shoota responded.

OG Jesse mean mugged the officer. "I can't wait to get out of here! I know you're going to be successful, son, and we don't have to subject ourselves to this shit no more!" He got angry because of the guard. "I'm tired of this shit anyway! It's time to do something different. You have my blessings, son. Now go hard on these bitches like we always do!" They gave each other a firm handshake to solidify the agreement.

"That's what I'm talking about, Dad. Don't you get tired of this shit?" Jason asked.

"Of course, but it's the life I chose." OG Jesse felt he had to live up to his reputation.

"Say no more, OG. I got this. When you come home I'll have a legal business set up for you to chill out with." D-Boy spoke with determination in his voice.

The rest of the visiting time was spent eating food, playing chess and cards. They briefly chatted about what was happening on the streets—who got killed, who got robbed, and who was snitching, the normal hood news.

"Okay, people! Visiting time is over!" the guard shouted.

"It was a pleasure meeting you, OG," Shoota said while shaking OG's hand.

"The pleasure is all mine, Shoota. Just keep doing what you do and together we will all make it to the top," OG said.

"I love you, Dad. I know they're going to release you this time." Jason hugged his father.

"Just be ready to live it up on some other shit this time." D-Boy hugged him too.

"I love you too, you're my soldiers. See you soon." OG always kept the goodbye's short. He slowly walked back to his cold, concrete and steel jail cell.

Shoota had a chance to understand D-Boy better from the visit. He saw the bond they shared with their father. It was something he always wished he had. It made him closer to D-Boy, ever since he'd witnessed the realness.

"I just want to thank you for bringing me on the visit. You're a real ass dude, and I thank God for putting you in my life. I'm as loyal as they come. I will never betray you! I don't have any family. You and Jason are like the only people that I can consider family. When you said you want to make this a family business, you're the closest thing to a family that I have. I'm happy to be a part of the family." Shoota spoke from the heart.

D-Boy and Jason both felt it.

"It's hard to find a loyal dude nowadays. Niggas be telling me that shit all the time, and they end up being pieces of shit. But I believe that you are a sincere dude, that's why I put the money up." Jason knew D-Boy was speaking the truth.

"I appreciate that, D. Word, we're going to shock the world!"

I'm going to see how loyal you really are, D-Boy thought. *I got some enemies that need to be shot, and you're the Shoota.*

D-Boy always had ulterior motives—it was never what it seemed with him. The reason he gave Shoota the money was to see if he would repay him by living up to his moniker. He used the trip to Attica to see if he could trust him. D-Boy's philosophy was, after sixteen hours of conversation, he'd know if you were built for what he was about to introduce you to. Shoota passed with flying colors.

D-Boy had a serious beef with the Haitian's that needed to be dealt with. He couldn't do it himself, because the Feds were watching him like a hawk, but they weren't watching Shoota. No one knew Shoota because all he did was record in the studio and sell and smoke weed. He was low-key, unlike D-Boy, and that's exactly why he chose Shoota.

"Let me ask you a serious question?" D-Boy parked the car. "You know that $10,000 you owe me? How would you like to put in some work to pay me back?" He pressed a button that revealed a highly concealed stash box located in the center console. In it was a Black Heckler & Koch automatic 9-millimeter handgun with two full clips and a silencer.

"Just point them out and say no more." That was all Shoota said to seal the deal.

"Take the 9-millimeter and the silencer. There is a clip already inserted, those two clips are just extras. It's all yours, tools for the job, know what I mean?" Shoota shook his head in compliance. "Tomorrow, I'll point them out."

Shoota took the items and concealed them on his person before he exited the vehicle. "I love you like a brother, D-Boy."

D-Boy nodded and stared Shoota dead in his eyes. "We'll see." That was all D-Boy said before he sped off.

On the way to Jason's apartment in Long Island, D-Boy was silent. He cranked up the sounds of Shoota's music as he did top speed on the Long Island Expressway. Jason didn't want to interrupt D-boy's thoughts because he had thoughts of his own. Like his safety. Jason always felt unsafe whenever he was in a car with his brother. They were shot at on two occasions, and Jason didn't care that his car was bulletproof, their bodies weren't.

They arrived at Jason's apartment in no time. "Come down to the station tomorrow. I'm going to blast off some of Shoota's new music."

"No doubt, after I take care of some business. See you tomorrow." He sped off as if he had somewhere important to be. D-Boy always drove like a maniac. He should've been a race car driver. During the drive, he had one person on his mind, Stephanie. They grew very close since New Year's Eve when she revealed her occupation.

"Call Steph," D-Boy commanded his car phone to dial her number.

Stephanie answered on the first ring, "Hey baby. How was the visit?"

"It was good. My father met Shoota and we had a great conversation."

"That's good. I miss you, baby."

"Not more than I miss you. I'm actually on my way to your apartment." He smiled to himself at the thought of seeing her.

"I'll be waiting for you in my birthday suit." She hung up.

D-Boy was so enamored by his thoughts that he didn't see one of his rivals from the Haitian mafia in a green minivan at the stop light. Usually, he'd circled the block before getting out, but he was so anxious that he pulled up in front of Stephanie's brownstone and then walked up to the door of building number 3717. The very beautiful Stephanie answered the door wearing a red silk robe.

D-Boy wasted no time walking inside and closing the door behind him. He grabbed Stephanie and kissed her as if starving for her passion. She responded by kissing him aggressively and removing her robe. D-Boy threw her on the couch and began to unbuckle his belt and remove his pants. Her green eyes burned with desire.

AMERICAN D - BOY

Like a bad B-rated thriller, someone kicked in the front door. Neither D-Boy nor Stephanie had time to make a move.

"I'm about to spoil all your fun," the Haitian man said as he cocked back his pistol.

Pop! Pop! Pop! Pop! Pop! Pop! Click! Click! Click! Click!

The shooter's fleeing footsteps brought D-Boy to reality. At the sound of the intruder's voice, D-Boy's first reaction was to drop to the floor and cover his head. He couldn't get to his weapon quick enough because his pants were down around hi

s ankles. Once the gunshots ended, he stood up to find Stephanie lying on the bullet riddled couch, dead with a bullet wound in her pretty head.

D-Boy held her lifeless body in his arms as he cried a river of tears onto her bleeding head. "No! No! No! Stephanie, don't go! Please get up, baby." He held her tighter and shook his head as if this wasn't really happening. "Why! She was a good woman. Why didn't you just take me?"

D-Boy held her until he heard sirens coming. *I have to get out of here.*

He quickly pulled up his pants and dashed to his Benz and sped off before the cops got to the scene. As he drove, tears streamed down his face so much his vision blurred.

"Word on everything I love! I'm going to destroy everything you touch for killing Stephanie!"

He knew who was responsible, and he blamed himself for slipping. D-Boy had gone outside of his regiment, and he paid the price for it.

89

ALAH ADAMS

"It's on now, bitches!"

CHAPTER 8

HOT 104 RADIO STATION

Jazzy strutted through Hot 104 radio station wearing designer shades, a new mink, and her engagement ring like she was an R&B diva. She knew she was being arrogant, but Jazzy didn't care. She had one person she wanted to see, Tracy. Tracy became Jazzy's mortal enemy.

There she goes, Jazzy thought. "Just the person I was looking for."

She approached Tracy. "I have some questions for you. Do you have a minute?"

"Sure." *What does this crazy bitch want today?* Tracy gave Jazzy a look of disdain.

"Since you're the Program Director, can you make sure my fiancé has six bottles of water, a veggie burger without cheese, 'cause my baby is a vegetarian. It's written in his contract that the station will provide lunch for him as an extra perk." Jazzy spoke in an annoying tone to get under Tracy's skin, and it was working.

"Listen, umm . . . Jessica." Tracy knew her real name.

"Jazzy, my name is Jazzy."

"Jazzy, Jessica, whatever. Listen, I am a Program Director, not an errand-girl or a go-for! I suggest you talk to DJ T-1. You two seem to have a good relationship. Whatever you do, please stay the fuck out of my face!" Tracy stormed to her office and slammed the door.

Jason watched the whole scene from the hallway, but remained hidden behind a wall listening to their female spat. Jazzy created the desired effect, which was getting under Tracy's skin. She didn't anticipate Tracy mentioning her and DJ T-1 in the same sentence. It caught her off-guard and Jason as well.

What does she know? Jazzy thought as she looked around to see if anyone else heard her snappy comeback.

Jason came walking out as if he wasn't there listening the whole time. "Hey baby."

"Oh, what's up, honey? I didn't see you over there."

"I was on my way to the DJ booth to do my show." He was holding a newspaper. "Did you hear what happened to D-Boy's girlfriend Stephanie?"

"No, what happened?"

"She was murdered at her apartment last night. I know D-Boy is fucked up about it. Damn, I feel sorry for him."

" My condolences go out to her family," Jazzy said.

"Mine too. I gotta give D-Boy a call once I'm done here. But I have to go get ready for the show." Jason kissed her on the cheek and headed for what he called his telephone booth. That's where Clark Kent went in to transform into Superman.

* * * * *

The day after the New Year's Eve party, word spread around the office that Jazzy and DJ T-1 were dancing very close. DJ T-1 had a reputation for sleeping with a lot of women from the station. D-Boy wasn't the only one who noticed. Tracy was going to save that card for a special occasion but she couldn't resist. What's done in the dark will always come to the light.

* * * * *

I have to be careful how I move, Jazzy thought as she headed toward DJ T-1's office. *But I have to pick up my money.*

She knocked on his door. "It's Jazzy, are you busy?"

"No, come in."

DJ T-1 got right down to business. He knew what she was there for. He opened a desk drawer and pulled out $25,000 in cash and handed it to Jazzy. "Fifty percent as promised. Here's $25,000 for the five songs you played."

Jazzy couldn't help smiling when she held the cold hard cash in her hands. She looked at DJ T-1 and the attraction showed on her face, and DJ T-1 noticed it.

She made a move to leave the office. "Slow down, baby. That's how you do a brother that handed you $25,000 just to have your little boyfriend play some songs? You have $25,000 coming to you every week for the next six months because of me. Can I at least take you out for dinner?"

Dinner was furthest from her mind; she was adding: *twenty-five thousand a week for the next six months. Let's see, that's one hundred thousand a month, so six months is six hundred thousand. You can have me for dinner for $600,000!*

Suddenly, the idea of having sex with DJ T-1 crossed her mind. She thought about the size of his manhood when she felt it on the dance floor. She closed her eyes and imagined it for a second. When she opened them, DJ T-1 was already on her like a cheap suit. He grabbed her in his arms and kissed her. At first she resisted, but resistance was futile. DJ T-1 knew he had Jazzy exactly where he wanted her. She gave in and kissed him back harder.

DJ T-1 felt her pelvis push up against his penis. He started unbuckling his Hermes belt and unbuttoned his pants. He held his penis in his hand, stroking it before he turned her around and lifted her mink. Jazzy pulled her tight designer jeans down around her ankles, then she poked her round ass out. He inserted his penis slow. With every stroke he increased his speed, until he was fucking her hard and fast.

"Yes! Fuck me!" Jazzy couldn't contain herself.

"You like that?" DJ T-1 asked.

"Yes! I love it! Keep fucking me with that big dick!" Jazzy yelled in ecstasy.

DJ T-1 was stroking her so hard and fast he couldn't pull out fast enough. He ejaculated on the back of Jazzy's new mink.

"You didn't cum in me, did you?" Jazzy asked desperately.

"Of course not. I got some on your mink though."

"What! How the fuck you do that?" Jazzy was furious. "Give me something to wipe it off with before it settles in!"

DJ T-1 handed her a towel. "My bad, I was too excited."

"Don't worry about it, it came off." *I can't believe I just did that.*

I knew I was going to tap that ass! That pussy good too! DJ T-1 thought.

"Don't worry, Jazzy. What happens between us stays between us. We getting money. Why not have a little pleasure in the meantime?" DJ T-1 kissed her.

"Please don't ever say anything. Jason would be devastated if he ever found out."

"I told you I got you. You better head out to the DJ booth. The show is on."

As soon as she exited the office, DJ T-1 grabbed a book from a small bookstand. There was a camera hidden in it taping the whole episode between him and Jazzy. He transferred the footage to his Samsung Galaxy.

DJ T-1 watched the footage, "Damn, I was tearing that pussy up if I do say so myself." He paused to reflect. "Everything is going better than planned." He watched the video three more times. "Revenge is so sweet."

ALAH ADAMS

CHAPTER 9

HAITIAN RESTAURANT
East New York, Brooklyn

Man, let me tell you, back in Haiti I had so many bitches! I had a bitch for every day of the month, you motherfucker! You can't tell me about no pussy!" Amos spoke with a heavy Haitian accent. He loved to talk about sex with his workers. "Speaking of pussy, what's the deal with this D-Boy? Why is he still alive?"

"This nigga be slipping through the fucking cracks. Bojo caught him last night, but he wasn't sure if he hit him. Every time we think we got him, that nigga gets away!" one of his bodyguards said.

"He can't keep getting lucky. He's not a fucking cat, and he doesn't have nine lives! I can't have this nigga taking food from my plate. Everyday he's alive I'm losing money, which means you're losing money!" Amos stabbed the plate with his fork.

A beautiful Haitian waitress walked up to the table with the bill. "Here's your bill, Mr. Amos." She smiled.

"Wait a minute, what's your name again?" Amos asked.

AMERICAN D - BOY

"Mina," she replied shyly.

"Write your name and number down for me. I want to take you out." He paid the bill and left a hundred dollar bill as a tip. "Don't spend it all in one spot. I'll call you." When she walked away, Amos said, "Now that's a nice young, firm piece of ass. I'm going to have fun with that."

Amos and his two bodyguards exited the restaurant to be greeted by a bum pushing a grocery cart. He had a scruffy beard and wore a dirty trench coat. "Please sir, can you spare a dollar?" The bum held his hand out.

"Get the fuck out of here!" Amos yelled as he pushed the cart out of his way and started walking toward his car with one of the guards following him.

The second bodyguard reached into his pocket to give the bum a dollar. "Here you go." Once he saw the silencer, it was too late. Shoota had already put two rounds in him so quick and silent that Amos kept walking to his car, oblivious that one of his bodyguards was down. Then he squeezed the trigger two more times and the other bodyguard dropped.

"What the fuck?" Those were the last words Amos spoke before Shoota unloaded the rest of the clip into his head and chest. He made sure Amos was dead.

"That was for Steph." Shoota knew how much D-Boy cared for her.

Shoota jogged around the block and snatched the fake beard off, then he took off the old dirty trench coat and threw both items into a dumpster. D-Boy was parked a half block up waiting for him. Shoota got in the passenger seat. "I made sure he was dead."

97

ALAH ADAMS

"Good, let's go to the radio station to see DJ T-1," D-Boy said calmly, as if nothing had happened.

As D-Boy pulled off, they saw police and heard ambulance sirens headed toward Shoota's small massacre. Shoota was out of breath, not from jogging but from the rush of adrenaline. This wasn't the first time he killed a man, but it was the first time he killed as a civilian. Shoota was an ex-marine, who served two tours in Afghanistan before he was honorably discharged. He was one of his platoon's best marksman, so they made him a sniper. He killed mostly local Taliban leaders that were holding anti-American rallies in small villages.

There was one kill that he would always regret, when he was ordered to assassinate an Arab teen. He began to protest, but he knew he had to follow orders, or it was his ass that would be in a sling. When he looked at the photo of his mark, it reminded him of himself when he was that age. They were the same cinnamon complexion, with features so similar they could pass for brothers.

On the day of the mission he had thoughts of abandoning it. Even the thought of disobeying orders made his stomach hurt. He had to do what he was programmed to do. So he set up his sniper rifle and got his target lined up in the scope, and that's when he saw the eyes of an innocent young man. *This kid isn't a terrorist, he's more like a young warrior fighting for his freedom, he thought.*

Shoota watched him for two minutes, then three minutes, and that's when he pulled the trigger. He knew the longer he watched him the more he would

98

have sympathy. As much as he hated to kill this teen, he felt like he had no choice. He was trained to kill without question or discretion. That was the last tour he signed up for, he just wanted out after that.

That kill affected Shoota so much that he swore off guns and violence altogether, until today. Images of killing the Arab teen flooded his mind, and he panted, having a panic attack!

"Yo! Shoota! Are you okay?" D-Boy saw him out of breath.

"I'm . . . okay. I just have . . . to get out of the car for a minute . . . to get some air," Shoota responded.

As soon as D-Boy pulled over, Shoota got out and threw his guts up all over the concrete. The emotions he kept bottled up, exploded in his mind causing him to have serious side effects. Shoota was suffering from a severe case of Post-Traumatic Stress Disorder.

D-Boy parked the car and went to a Bodega to get Shoota some water. He drank it down in three gulps.

"I need something stronger." There was a liquor store on the corner.

"Do you like D'ussé?" D-Boy asked.

"I never heard of it, but fuck it I'll try it." Shoota sat back in the passenger seat.

The rest of the ride to the station was silent, no music and no talking, just thoughts.

That feels better. I just needed to get the cobwebs out of my system. This D'ussé is making me feel invincible! This shit is better than Henny! I'm ready to go on a fucking killing spree! Shoota took big swigs of the strong cognac while in thought.

D-Boy watched Shoota closely. *This nigga drinking that D'ussé like its Hawaiian Punch. I think I just created a monster! I have to keep this dude under control.*

They pulled up to the radio station and got out to enter the building. Shoota was swaying from drinking so much alcohol, but he wasn't stumbling. As soon as they stepped into the building, they bumped into Jazzy coming out of DJ T-1's office. She hid her suspicious eyes behind the large, dark Versace glasses she wore.

"Hey, what's up, D-Boy?" she said nervously as she made her way thru the hall headed toward Jason's DJ station.

"What up, Jazzy?" D-Boy noticed she was walking fast.

"You know her?" Shoota asked. "That's a nice fucking mink! She paid some money for that."

"Yeah, I know her. That's my brother's girl . . . I mean fiancée. He bought her that mink. If it was up to me I wouldn't have bought her sneaky ass shit!" D-Boy glanced back at her, and he noticed a stain on the back of her mink. *What the fuck is that?*

When they reached DJ T-1's office and knocked, no one answered. "That's strange. Jazzy just came out of this office," D-Boy said.

"Hold on!" DJ T-1 said as it took him a moment to open the door. "Oh, what's up, Shoota?" He didn't acknowledge D-Boy until they entered the office.

"What's up? DJ T-1." T-1 introduced himself and gave D-Boy a handshake.

"They call me D-Boy." He kept it brief.

"This is my new manager. He'll be handling all my business from now on," Shoota said.

"Okay, that's what's up." *Where do I know this nigga from? Oh yeah, that's the nigga that was staring me down at the New Year's Eve party.* DJ T-1 caught eye contact with D-Boy.

"Shoota was telling me that you have a two for one deal for him on the next go around," D-Boy said.

"Yes! Shoota is shooting up the charts! He came in at number one in the rap category on iTunes, and they want to hear more!" DJ T-1 was genuinely surprised. "Out of all the new artists we debuted that day, Shoota and Top Notch are the most requested."

D-Boy pulled out a brick of money and laid it on the desk. "That's ten racks. We'll have the music for you by Friday."

DJ T-1 put the money in his desk drawer. "I can't wait to hear your new music. The Program Director has been bugging me about getting some new music from you."

"It's coming, and it's coming hard! You feel me!" Shoota was feeling himself.

"Let's go!" DJ T-1 was hyped.

"We're on our way to the studio when we leave here," Shoota said.

"Don't let me hold you up. I have some business to take care of in ten minutes. I'll see you guys Friday. Nice to meet you, D-Boy."

"The pleasure was all mine," D-Boy responded smoothly.

They exited the office and stopped by the DJ booth to see Jason. Jazzy was rubbing his shoulders when they entered. She kept her dark Versace shades on as a mask. D-Boy glanced at her skeptically. He knew something wasn't right with her. *If it looks fishy and smells fishy, it's fishy!*

D-Boy felt her staring at him through the shades.

"What's up, Jay?" D-Boy said while giving his brother a hug and handshake.

"I'm sorry to hear about what happened to Stephanie. I know you were getting serious with her ," Jason said with concern.

D-Boy had to hold back tears. "She was the only woman I ever loved." He paused to catch his composure. "But I didn't come down here for that."

"What up, Shoota? You ready to do it again?" Jason asked in an attempt to change the subject.

"We about to drop two more singles on Friday!" Shoota responded.

"Wow! I can't believe my little brother is managing one of the hottest new artists in NYC!" Jason was happy because D-Boy never expressed an interest in anything other than hustling.

"I'm so sorry about what happened to Stephanie," Jazzy said with a sympathetic look, but she instantly changed the topic. "And ummm, Congratulations, D-Boy. I know you're going to make a good manager." Her stomach churned with despair. Soon he would be asking his brother questions.

"Thank you, Jazzy. I just wanted to stop in to say what's up. We're on our way to the studio." D-Boy turned his attention to Jason. "But I do want to talk to you when you get a chance. It's about Dad," D-Boy said.

"Is he all right?" Jason was concerned.

"He's good. I just have to tell you some personal family business."

Jason shook his hand. "Okay, I'll call you after I finish my set at Club Delight."

"Talk to you later." D-Boy looked at Jazzy as he exited.

"Are you okay, baby?" Jason asked.

"I'm okay. Why do you ask?"

"You've been very quiet today, that's not like you. You always have something to *school* me on." Jason smiled.

"I was just listening. Sometimes it's better to be observant." She couldn't shake the guilt eating her from inside.

"Isn't that great! My brother is finally getting his life together. Shoota is the most requested artist in NYC!" Jason was genuinely excited for D-Boy.

"I'm happy for him. I'm proud of him. Maybe I can give him some tips," Jazzy added.

"That's why I love you. You're always thinking of the team. That'll bring you two closer. I want that because you and my brother are the two most important people in my life." He knew they didn't get along.

"No doubt." Jazzy hugged him tightly. "You know I love you right, Jason?"

"Of course, baby." Jason put on his leather coat. "You ready? Let's blow this popsicle stand."

"Let me use the bathroom before we leave."

Jazzy dashed to the bathroom as if she had to relieve her bowels, but she really had to relieve her soul. As soon as she entered the stall she removed the glasses and tears flowed from her eyes non-stop. She couldn't control it. She hated to betray Jason, but she felt she was in too deep to turn back and that's what hurt her most. Jazzy cried until her eyesight blurred, then she reached into her Hermès Birkin bag and grabbed the stacks of cash. *I'm going to buy me a brand new Birkin bag tomorrow to make me feel better.*

She exited the stall and stopped to wash her hands and throw some water on her tears. She looked at her reflection, and she didn't like what she saw. Yet she smiled, then put the dark Versace shades back on and left the bathroom.

CHAPTER 10

DJ T-1'S HOUSE
Hollis, Queens

Damn, son! You was digging shorty out!" Jermaine said.

DJ T-1 smiled. "That's what I do, my nigga!"

DJ T-1 had a collection of thirty-six videos of him having sex with women. None of the women knew they were being taped, that's what made it creepy. He showed his closest friend Jermaine every one of them. DJ T-1 got some kind of satisfaction from secretly filming women. It made him feel like more of a man to be able to seduce women and tape them without them knowing. DJ T-1's philosophy was, if they don't know they're being filmed, they will give a natural performance.

"You're a fucking pimp! How do you get these bitches to fuck you like that in your office every time?" Jermaine was in awe.

"I just got skills, my nigga. One day I'll show you how it's done firsthand," DJ T-1 said jokingly.

"Fuck out of here! You trying to play me now, my nigga!" Jermaine threw DJ T-1 a playful punch.

"I'm just fucking with you. But seriously though, this cat came in the office today named D-Boy. You know when you know someone, but you can't remember how you know them, or where you know them from?" DJ T-1 couldn't get D-Boy out of his mind.

"Did you say D-Boy?" Jermaine asked with a serious expression.

"Yeah D-Boy. He manages that new cat, Shoota." DJ T-1 was curious to see where his line of questioning was going.

"Everybody in the hood knows who the fuck D-Boy is, my nigga! Where the fuck you been?" Jermaine replied.

"Excuse me if I have better things to do than to sell drugs all day in the hood," DJ T-1 replied sarcastically.

"You remember about two years ago they arrested this guy for murder and drugs. He owned almost every business on Queens Boulevard. He was only twenty years old or something, so the news was calling him the 'baby face gangster.'"

"I do remember hearing about that. He had a lot of charges, and I think he beat them all in trial or something like that."

"He beat all the charges! D-Boy is the biggest drug dealer, slash killer, slash pimp, extortionist—you name it he does it! He is not to be fucked with. The man has murdered about ten people in the hood, and that's the ones I know of." Jermaine spoke of D-Boy like he was a street legend.

"That explains why I feel like I've seen him before! I do remember seeing his face on the news! He put that money up for Shoota." DJ T-1 was putting two and two together. "He didn't look like a killer. He looked more like a pimp or a player—not a killer."

"I'm telling you, don't sleep on him. He has a reputation for flipping out for no reason and busting shots at whoever. He don't give a fuck who he kills, and he gets away with it."

"You talking about him like he Super-Nigga or somebody! He can get killed too, if he fuck around with the wrong nigga!" DJ T-1 took the gun from under the couch and cocked it. "He fuck with me, and I'll body that little nigga!"

"You asked who he was and I told you." Jermaine wasn't impressed by DJ T-1's gangster performance.

"I'll be right back." DJ T-1 left to use the bathroom.

Jermaine saw the phone sitting on the coffee table. He picked it up and saw that the video of Jazzy was on pause. Cautiously, he looked around and listened for footsteps before he made his move. He sent the video to his phone. The download was taking seconds to complete. "Come on, hurry up!" Jermaine said to himself.

Just as it was finishing, DJ T-1 was coming back. "Everything cool? I thought I heard you talking to someone."

"I was on the phone. I'm about to go see this shorty on the South Side. I'll see you tomorrow, my nigga," Jermaine said.

"Be safe, my nigga," DJ T-1 said suspiciously, wondering why he was leaving so fast.

Jermaine waited until he was in his car to make sure the video was successfully downloaded to his phone. "Yes! I can blackmail the hell out of him with this video."

Jermaine recalled all the times that DJ T-1 bragged about all the money he was getting at Hot 104. DJ T-1 made the mistake of telling his business to the wrong person. He told Jermaine everything, including the list of artists who were paying him $10,000 to get their songs played. Jermaine also knew it was illegal to take money to play records. He wouldn't have known anything if T-1 didn't tell him.

As he drove, Jermaine thought of T-1's nice home, brand new black BMW 750i, and the expensive designer clothes he always wore all year round. *Shit, why shouldn't I extort DJ T-1? I know he got it, and I need a come-up. A nigga tired of this hustling shit! I'm trying to live large too!*

The truth was, Jermaine was jealous of DJ T-1. He pretended to like him, but he was a genuine hater! He hated the fact that he couldn't live like DJ T-1, with money and fame. Everyone in NYC knew who DJ T-1 was, but no one knew Jermaine. DJ T-1 made hundreds of thousands easily without breaking a sweat, while Jermaine had to risk his life and his freedom to make a couple thousand.

Behind his back, Jermaine talked about DJ T-1 like a dog. "DJ T-1 is so lame! He getting all this money and he be tricking on strippers, buying pussy! I only fuck with the lame because he gets me passes to all the hot concerts. Other than that I wouldn't even call him." Jermaine often spoke like this about DJ T-1 to others.

If you asked DJ T-1 who one of his closest friends was, he'd quickly say Jermaine. If he knew what Jermaine was saying about him, he'd want to put a bullet in his head. He knew Jermaine from his hustling days, and even back then DJ T-1 was getting money. Jermaine had forgotten, but he used to work for DJ T-1 briefly. Jermaine was always a hater, that's why he'd always be a bench warmer and not a player.

When Jermaine left DJ T-1, he sat back thinking about what he told him concerning D-Boy. It brought back memories of when he was in the drug game. DJ T-1 used to be one of the biggest drug dealers in the hood until he became a DJ. In fact, the reason he became a DJ was to get out of the game. After he was shot and his little brother was killed, DJ T-1 left the game and pursued something legal.

He was searching for the perfect idea that would substitute hustling. It had to be something that would bring in just as much money as the drug game. He looked desperately for the next hustle that wasn't as dangerous.

"Fuck it, I might as well get used to just selling drugs for the rest of my life." He was about to give up until he got a call from an old friend named DJ Threat.

"Tell me that you still get busy on the wheels of steel?" DJ Threat asked.

"Of course, that's something I'll never lose. I was nicer than you back in the day," DJ T-1 responded.

"I have an opportunity for you. I need a dude that can really DJ, to hold me down as my backup DJ when I go on breaks and vacations."

"Definitely! I'm down, my nigga!" DJ T-1 was ecstatic.

His good fortune was met with some obstacles that would keep him in the game. Come to find out, the real reason DJ Threat wanted DJ T-1 as his assistant was because he had a drug habit. He knew that T-1 sold drugs, so he asked him for coke every time he needed him at the station. The more coke he gave DJ Threat, the more he worked at the station.

DJ T-1 went along with the program and gave Threat drugs in exchange for the opportunity to DJ at a major radio station. Eventually, DJ Threat couldn't keep up the façade and the drugs got the best of him. One day he lit himself on fire smoking crack in the bathroom. That's when the station fired him and hired DJ T-1 in his place. That was ten years ago.

"Where is my phone?" DJ T-1 asked, looking around. "I thought I put it down on the coffee table. Why is it on the couch?" He picked it up and examined it. The video of Jazzy was the last thing on it.

"Video sent successfully!" He looked inside his messages and saw that he sent the video of Jazzy to Jermaine. "That sneaky son-of-a-bitch! I knew there was a reason he ran out of here so fast!"

AMERICAN D-BOY

He immediately called Jermaine. "What the fuck is up with you, son?" DJ T-1 was furious.

"What you mean?" Jermaine was laughing on the other end.

"You know what the fuck I mean! You got the video of me and shorty in your phone, and I want that shit deleted now! Or you got some serious problems!"

"Oh word, I got some serious problems. Nigga, suck my dick! You the one that has serious problems!" Jermaine's tone turned serious. "I want $100,000 by Friday, or this video goes on World Star Hip Hop and the Feds will be at your door on Saturday morning with a warrant for your arrest." Jermaine hung up the phone.

DJ T-1 went into panic mode. "What the fuck am I going to do? This nigga can really screw me."

He pulled up the footage and looked at it again for the hundredth time. He wasn't just having sex. The video started with DJ T-1 incriminating himself by giving her $25,000. "Fifty percent as promised. Here's $25,000 for the five songs you played." That wasn't it. As he watched, he incriminated himself more by saying, *"Slow down, baby. That's how you do a brother that handed you $25,000 just to have your little boyfriend play some songs. You got $25,000 coming to you every week for the next six months because of me. Can I at least take you out for dinner?"*

After viewing the evidence stacked against him, he just dropped to the floor. "I'm fucked! I might as well give him the fucking money, or lose everything I worked hard for and go to prison."

He couldn't think of any other alternative, then it hit him like a sledge hammer. He thought about what Jermaine said about D-Boy. *The man has murdered about ten people in the hood, and that's the ones I know of.*

"I got a direct link to D-Boy through Shoota. Why not give him less than half of that $100,000 to murder your bitch-ass!" DJ T-1 smiled. "Matter of fact, why not play his records to have you killed. It'll cost me nothing to have you washed up, Jermaine."

Those devious thoughts put DJ T-1 at ease. He lit up a Commodore cigar, something he liked to do when he was stressed. DJ T-1 was no stranger to beef—he actually used to welcome it. Jermaine just woke up the beast in DJ T-1.

Actually, he was hurt by Jermaine's actions. He regarded him as a close friend. There were many times DJ T-1 gave Jermaine money and helped him out.

"All the concert tickets I gave this ungrateful ass nigga!" He took a healthy puff of the expensive cigar. "So you want to fuck with me! Let's play the game then!"

* * * * *

"Are you ready to order?" the waitress asked, interrupting Jason's conversation with Sam.

"I'll have the jerk chicken dinner," Jason said.

"I'll just have the same thing he's having." Sam replied.

"Now you see why I said you had to pay close attention to the story," Jason said

"This shit is getting crazier by the minute," Sam said.

"I know, and the crazy part about it is, I didn't even get to the good part yet," Jason responded.

"This shit sounds more entertaining than a blockbuster movie."

"Only difference is, this shit is real life."

Jason looked at Sam, and for some reason he reminded him of someone. It was like he'd seen him before, but he couldn't remember where.

"What's wrong? Did I do something?" Sam asked, noticing Jason's expression.

"No, I just had a thought, that's all."

I hope he didn't notice me. It's too early to blow my cover, Sam thought.

ALAH ADAMS

CHAPTER 11

MUSIC PALACE RECORDING STUDIOS
Hempstead, New York

his guy is awesome!" the engineer said while Shoota was in the microphone booth recording his verse.

"I only mess with the best!" D-Boy was excited about Shoota's new song.

Shoota was rapping with more confidence and swag ever since he got with D-Boy. He was evolving into a great artist. D-Boy liked the idea of getting out of the game and just managing Shoota once the money got bigger. D-Boy knew he was wanted by the alphabet boys: FBI, ATF, DEA, and NYPD. He always stayed seven steps ahead of them. Now was the opportune time to get out of the streets.

When he was finished with his song, Shoota exited the booth. "How'd I sound?" he asked.

"You sounded great! Better than a lot of the stuff I record in here," the engineer said.

"What do you think, D-Boy?" Shoota valued D-boy's opinion more than anyone's.

"I think it's better than the 'New John Gotti,' and that shit is all over the radio!" D-Boy was turned up.

"That's what up! I'm ready to record another song."

"Let's go!" the engineer said.

D-Boy's phone rang. It was Jason. "What's up, big bro?"

"You tell me. What's going on with Dad?" Jason was concerned. Even though he wasn't close to his father like D-Boy was, he still cared for him.

"Is Jazzy around?" D-Boy asked. He didn't want her to hear his conversation because it pertained to her.

"Yes, she's right here. Why?"

"I want to catch you by yourself. How about we meet tomorrow at Hot 104?" D-Boy asked.

"That's cool," Jason responded. "See you tomorrow . . ." He hung up the phone. *I wonder why D-Boy seems so suspicious of Jazzy.*

* * * * *

"Baby, let me ask you a question," Jason said to Jazzy. "What's going on with you and my brother? I thought that you guys were cool after that incident."

"We are. Why do you ask?" Jazzy knew that D-Boy was on the phone, and Jason's line of questioning was about that call. *I hope this isn't what I think it is.*

"He doesn't want to talk about anything around you. He asked me if you were around just now, like he didn't want you to hear the conversation."

"I don't know what's going on in his head. You know your brother is crazy, who knows." She threw him off by stating the obvious, because D-Boy was crazy.

"You're right, baby. Who knows what's up with
him?" Jason gave her a kiss on the forehead. "I love
you, Jazzy."

"I love you too, baby," she responded.

*Something is wrong and I'm going to find out
what it is. I always do,* Jason thought.

MUSIC PALACE RECORDING STUDIOS

Two FBI agents sat in an unmarked car outside of
Music Palace studios waiting for D-Boy to come out.
They had been following him all week based on the tip
from an informant. Apparently, one of D-Boy's
workers got caught, and instead of doing time, he
decided to snitch on his boss.

"This guy D-Boy is a rapper now or something?
What the fuck is he doing in the studio all the time?"
Agent Kowalski asked.

"Be patient, partner. Whatever he's doing in there
has nothing to do with the investigation. We can't lose
him this time. This guy is always slipping, not this
time," Senior Agent Trenton responded.

Agent Trenton had been tracking D-Boy since he
was eighteen. In fact, he was the arresting officer for
D-Boy's first case. It was a drug case. They thought
they had enough evidence to put D-Boy away for
twenty years. But D-Boy beat all the charges by killing
all the witnesses, which left a bad taste in Agent
Trenton's mouth. One of D-Boy's latest victims was
Stephanie, or so they thought. What D-Boy didn't
know was that Agent Trenton and Stephanie used to be
in a relationship. Because he thought D-Boy murdered

Steph, he vowed to get enough evidence to send D-Boy away for life.

D-Boy knew they were out there. He always knew when they were following him. Today he was going to try something out of the ordinary. He learned something valuable from OG Jesse: "Go at your enemy head on. They'll never expect it."

He put on his waist length white and gray Chinchilla and headed outside. Shoota was in the booth recording. "I'll be right back," D-Boy said to the engineer.

D-Boy exited the building and looked around for a vehicle that looked like an unmarked FBI vehicle with two out of place white guys sitting in it. "There they go!" He walked toward their vehicle.

They watched him as he got closer. "Is he coming over to us right now?" the junior officer asked in a panic. "Fuck! Our fucking cover is blown! Let's get out of here before he sees us."

"Shut the fuck up, Agent Kowalski! Let his black ass come over here all he wants. It's a free country. As long as he doesn't break the law I won't break his spirit," Agent Trenton said.

D-Boy strolled over to the Federal agents as cool as the chill in the winter air. He took a roll of the dice with this action. It could cost him his life if he made the wrong move. In D-Boy's mind, this was his defining moment, not to intimidate them but to use reverse psychology.

He stopped short of the driver's side and made a motion with his hand for them to roll the window down. "Good evening, officers. It's chilly as hell out here tonight, so I won't waste much of your time."

Agent Trenton got out of the car. "I love the cold. What is it that you'd like to say to us, Darius? Oh, I forgot, I meant D-Boy?" Trenton said cynically.

"First, let me start by saying that I'm not a criminal, and I know you're just doing your job, but you're truly wasting your time. Look at you, sitting here in a cold ass car with the engine turned off waiting on me to do something incriminating. I'm in the music business, everything is legit," D-Boy said with confidence.

"Yeah right. I guess I'm Tweedle Dee and my partner is Tweedle Dum," Agent Kowalski said with off-beat delivery.

D-Boy and Agent Trenton both gave Agent Kowalski a peculiar look. "That might be very well what you're doing, now. We know for a fact that you weren't just in the music business a year ago. You were involved with a number of shady businesses. And I know personally that you had something to do with Stephanie's murder! You black son-of-a-bitch!" Agent Trenton lost it for a second, but he brought it back down. "I can't prove that, but we both know she was about to take the witness stand against you before you had her killed."

"Listen, I don't know anything about Stephanie's murder. I didn't know you had this much love for Stephanie." D-Boy struck a chord on Agent Trenton's heartstring with that statement.

"You got some balls waltzing over here with your fancy fur coat and your expensive jewelry. You have no right telling me anything about Stephanie. I promise you this, D-Boy. When I'm done, you'll have to live the rest of your life in a prison cell, where you will die."

D-Boy tilted his head to both sides, cracking his neck bones before speaking. "And I promise you this—I'll leave this earth in a pine box before you ever get the chance to achieve your malicious goal. I'm sorry that Stephanie got killed, but that's how life goes. We all have to die one day. She was living a dangerous life." D-Boy stared at Agent Trenton dead in his eyes without blinking. "That's all I have to say. Good night, gentlemen." D-Boy walked back to the studio.

The conversation was fruitful for both sides. D-Boy understood why Agent Trenton wanted his head on a platter. Stephanie was falling in love with D-Boy. After his experience with Stephanie, D-Boy never let women in and that's when he became like a pimp. He was actually going to marry Stephanie and get out of the game. She wanted to retire and be with D-Boy, but she was killed before she could make that move.

"So they really want my head now. Interesting," D-Boy said to himself as he entered the building.

For Agent Trenton, it gave him another angle to trap D-Boy. He had a hunch that D-Boy was doing something in the music business that was breaking some law. He knew there was a lot of illegal activity in the rap music business. He just had to connect D-Boy to one of those activities and he had him.

"You're going to slip up, and I'll be right there to put your smug ass away for good." Agent Trenton got in the car and started it. "Get in the fucking car, Kowalski!" Kowalski was standing in the same spot.

He rushed to the passenger side, and they rode off into the night, scheming.

* * * * *

"Here you go," the waitress announced as she placed the steaming hot plates in front of Jason and Sam. "Enjoy."

"Thank you," Jason said.

"Those FBI agents sound like real assholes," Sam said.

"They were more than just assholes. They were racist assholes that had it out for a young black brother."

"They're the worst, especially when you give them power," Sam added.

"Power, that's what it's all about at the end of the day." Jason dug into his plate with a vengeance. He hadn't eaten all day.

"So is that the end of this adventurous journey?" Sam asked, knowing the answer to his own question.

"It's far from over. The best part is coming up."

CHAPTER 12

HOT 104 RADIO STATION

It's your boy, DJ Jay-Roc on the wheels of steel! This next joint is from a new artist named Rick Rude. He's been lighting up the scene with his new song 'Ticket to the Moon!' You heard it here first on Hot 104 where trends are set! Let's get it!" Jason announced in his signature voice before debuting the record.

Jazzy sat in the booth with him today, which was rare.

"Are you okay, Jazzy?" he asked with concern.

"Why you ask?"

"Your face looks flush, like you're about to vomit or something."

"Excuse me, I have to go to the ladies room for a minute."

As soon as she entered the stall, Jazzy stuck her head near the toilet and threw up her guts. She had been feeling sick every morning for two weeks now. She just kept it to herself. Jazzy knew her body, something was wrong. She didn't want to ask herself the million dollar question: Can her sickness be due to a pregnancy?

She walked out of the stall to see Tracy standing at the mirror putting on lip stick. "Someone is sick, glad it isn't me. I heard you in there throwing up. I thought it was someone else," Tracy said in an arrogant tone.

"Why don't you ever mind your business?" Jazzy didn't even have enough strength to put up a good fight.

"Listen, Jazzy, I think we got off on the wrong foot. How about we start over? I don't have anything against you," Tracy said.

"I don't trust females like you. I see the way you look at my man. I'll be damned if I just sit there and be phony and pretend to like you when I don't," Jazzy said with venom.

"Well, excuse me. At least I tried."

"And you failed." Jazzy exited the bathroom.

To her surprise, when she stepped into the booth D-Boy was already there having a conversation with Jason. She had to listen to get caught up to speed. Luckily for her, D-Boy was telling him about his conversation with the Feds last night. They were still feeling salty about Stephanie's murder.

"That's crazy! I remember how you really liked her," Jason recalled. "She was your boo thang."

"I was about to make her my wife." D-Boy had to look away to keep from getting emotional.

"It's all right little brother."

"I wish things were different, but that's just the hand I was dealt." D-Boy resented what happened to Stephanie. He knew those bullets were meant for him.

"Anyway, what's up with Dad?" Jason asked.

AMERICAN D-BOY

"I need to speak to my brother alone. Can you excuse us?" D-Boy asked Jazzy.

"No, anything you have to say about OG is going to be repeated to me, so why not save yourself the energy," Jazzy responded in a nasty tone.

"First of all, who the fuck are you talking to like that? Yo Jay, check your bitch!" D-Boy spoke with a snarl.

Jason frowned. "No, she's right. I'm tired of this bullshit between you two! She's my fiancée, my future wife. Anything you can say to me you can say in front of her."

"Word? It's like that! You know what, fuck both of you!" D-Boy stormed out of the booth.

On his way to the elevator, D-Boy ran into DJ T-1. "D-Boy! Let me holler at you in my office for a minute," DJ T-1 said. "It'll only take a minute of your time."

D-Boy was hesitant, but he stepped into DJ T-1's office. "What's good?"

"I have a little problem I need taken care of." DJ T-1 spoke in codes that he thought D-Boy would know.

"What kind of problem?" D-Boy asked with resignation.

"An extermination situation."

"Rats or roaches?" D-Boy's question was also an answer.

"It's a bit of both, but I was told that you have the resources to get rid of my little problem tonight." DJ T-1 was desperate.

"You got $10,000 and it's a done deal," D-Boy said.

DJ T-1 reached into his drawer and pulled out $10,000 as if he was pulling a rabbit out of a hat. "This is a picture of my problem." DJ T-1 showed D-Boy a pic of Jermaine on his phone and slid the money toward D-Boy.

D-Boy looked at the picture and made a familiar expression. *I know this dude! That's Jermaine from 109th. He used to work for me, but he didn't know it.*

"This nigga was my boy until he violated. All I want is his phone after you take care of him. Make sure you get his phone. He has something in it that I need." Perspiration dripped down DJ T-1's head.

"Whatever, just give me the time and location and I'll have it done." D-Boy was about to say something until he remembered. "Oh yeah, Shoota has those two songs ready to roll tomorrow as promised."

"Okay, I can't wait to hear them. This is the place and time he'll be expecting me." DJ T-1 handed D-Boy a piece of paper.

"Consider it done." D-Boy walked out of the building before calling Shoota. "What up, Shoota? I got a little job for you."

That's all he had to say to get Shoota's killer wheels turning. "Say no more."

When D-Boy hung up, he thought about the argument he just had with Jason. He'd only had two real arguments with his brother in his whole life, this one made the third. He hated that Jason took Jazzy's side after she spoke to him like that. He couldn't believe they had argued because of a bitch. D-Boy would never let one of his girls talk crazy to Jason. The G check would've been immediate. Jazzy had Jason wrapped around her finger. He wondered how Jason would feel if he saw how Jazzy was dancing all up on DJ T-1 on New Year's Eve. Surely she had the wool pulled over his eyes. But from now on, D-Boy decided to mind his own business. *Whatever happens between them two happens.*

His thoughts turned to Jermaine. He was never one to jump into anything. Contrary to what everyone believed, D-Boy was a thinker.

I remember Jermaine. He was a good worker. I wonder what he did to DJ T-1? I know for sure DJ T-1 isn't going to tell me, so I might as well ask Jermaine.

D-Boy could get in contact with any hustler in the city through a busy body chick named Tasia. She had Jermaine's number. If she didn't, she knew someone in the hood that did. Tasia was also D-Boy's personal spy. She kept her eyes and ears open for anyone opposing D-Boy's rule. That's how he knew who to take out and who to let live.

"Tasia, get Jermaine's number for me," D-Boy ordered.

"Jermaine from 109th?" Tasia asked.

"Yeah, that Jermaine."

"I got his number. I be buying weed from him sometimes. Hold on, baby." Tasia went through her list of contacts. She had him listed under *Grimy Ass Jermaine.* "The number is 646-246-7656. He's going to answer because that's his trap phone."

"Good looking, Tasia."

"Oh yeah, I forgot to tell you, the Feds was all up in the projects yesterday asking about you. Like what you up to nowadays and stuff like that. Be careful out there, D-Boy."

"I will. Good looking for everything. I appreciate you, Tasia."

"You welcome, boo-boo." Tasia hung up.

D-Boy dialed the number that Tasia gave him. Jermaine picked up on the first ring. "It's Maine, who's this?"

"What up, my nigga? This is D-Boy," D-Boy said in a befriending tone.

"The D-Boy? Stop playing, Morris. I know this is you. What you want, Morris?" Jermaine was serious. This couldn't be D-Boy.

"Nah, my nigga, this isn't Morris. This is D-Boy! Jamaica Queens finest! Don D-Boy himself." D-Boy knew once he ran off his list of monikers Jermaine would know he was the real deal.

"What's really good with you, my G? The last time I saw you, you was flossing at the Queens Center mall in the white Benz! What can I do for you, my nigga?" Jermaine was a true fan of D-Boy's. D-Boy was whom Jermaine aspired to be, a successful hustler. Not every hustler is successful.

"Meet me by the Coliseum mall in half an hour. I got to ask you something that I can't mention on the phone. It's some good bread in it for you too." D-Boy knew that money was the greatest motivator for a low level street hustler like Jermaine.

"My nigga, you won't believe this! I'm at the Coliseum mall right now! Come thru. I'm here, my nigga, like a loyal fucking soldier!" Jermaine was amped. He thought this was his lucky day to get a call from D-Boy.

"I'm about to pull up in front. Come outside and get in."

D-Boy was around the corner, but he always liked to circle the block before he came through the hood. He pulled up to the front. Jermaine was outside talking to some other low level hustlers.

"I'll check y'all niggas out later. My nigga D-Boy came through to pick me up." Jermaine was fronting like gold teeth and they knew it. Every day he was out on the avenue selling dime bags of weed with them. "I'll check y'all out tomorrow." He got in the Benz. "What up, D-Boy?"

"Listen, I'm getting straight to business. Somebody wants you dead, and you have to be smart in how you answer these questions." D-Boy was very serious.

Jermaine almost shit his pants from the fear that just came over him. He knew that D-Boy was serious, but he couldn't think of anyone on D-Boy's level he had beef with. "Whatever you want to know, D-Boy. I don't want no problems with you, my nigga." Jermaine was almost trembling.

"You know DJ T-1? What did you do to him?"

"Oh, you talking about bitch ass DJ T-1! He mad because I sent myself a video of him fucking some chick in his office. His scary ass is talking about getting me killed because of that!" Jermaine wanted to laugh.

"Let me see the video," D-Boy demanded.

Jermaine didn't hesitate to show D-Boy the video. When he saw Jazzy come in the office with the mink, he knew the exact day this video was taken.

"Here is the $25,000 for the five songs just like I promised," DJ T-1 said.

D-Boy thought, *that answers my question about the money. This bitch has been getting paid behind my brother's back!*

"Slow down, baby. That's how you do a brother that handed you $25,000 just to have your little boyfriend play some songs? You got $25,000 coming to you every week for the next six months because of me. Can I at least take you out for dinner?" DJ T-1 said.

Then came the part that turned D-Boy's stomach. He watched his brother's fiancé getting fucked, the same woman that made Jason rise up against him. The finale came when DJ T-1 ejaculated some of his cum on the back of her fur.

He was so disgusted that he took the phone from Jermaine's hand. "Here's $500 for this phone. Go get yourself another one."

"But I have all my connections in that phone!" Jermaine almost cried.

"Here's another $500 for your troubles. Who else did you show this video to?" D-Boy stared in his eyes to see if he was telling the truth.

"Just a couple of my mans' from the block. Those niggas ain't nobody important. Don't worry, this video didn't go on the Internet. I didn't send it to anybody. Only four people, and you—that makes five people in the whole world that saw it, honestly." Jermaine knew he better tell the truth or he could wind up dead.

D-Boy believed him. "Go see Tasia. She's going to be your pick up spot from now on. You work for me now." D-Boy drove off. *This is some foul ass shit.*

He hated to be right about Jazzy, because it meant crushing his brother's heart. He always had a feeling that Jazzy was scandalous. Maybe it was the way she gazed at other men when she thought he wasn't paying attention. Whatever it was, D-Boy was right. That was an advantage he had over his brother. Street smarts.

D-Boy was so upset that he shed tears just thinking about the pain Jason was going to endure when he saw the video. He knew Jason was a good man, and he definitely didn't deserve this. He had worked hard all his life to avoid negativity, and the one person Jason loved was deceiving him.

He's going to be devastated when he finds out, but he has to see it to free himself from Jazzy's hold. Sometimes you have to fall down to come up, something Grandpa Joe told me a long time ago. I guess it's true.

D-Boy called DJ T-1. "It's done." He had other plans for DJ T-1, who didn't know he and Jason were brothers. But he would soon find out in the worse way.

ALAH ADAMS

CHAPTER 13

FBI FIELD OFFICE
Downtown Brooklyn, New York

There were pictures of Jason on the folder that read:
SUSPECT: Jason 'DJ Jay-Roc' Jensen.
CHARGES: 5 COUNTS OF CRIMINAL
ENTERPRISE OF FEDERAL PROPERTY.

The Feds owned everything, even the airwaves that radio stations use to broadcast music. They were building a case on Jason from the day he played the first five songs on the radio. He made himself a suspect of an on-going Federal investigation at Hot 104.

An agent that was deep undercover posing as a rap artist paid $10,000 to have his song played on Hot 104. He paid the fee five more times until the supervisor told him they had enough evidence to issue an arrest warrant for Jason 'DJ Jay-Roc' Jensen.

DJ T-1 made a copy of Jason's application and started a PayPal account under the name DJ Jay-Roc. He instructed the artist to wire the money to the DJ Jay-Roc account so there was no meeting in person. As far as the Feds knew, DJ T-1 or Jazzy had nothing to do with this elaborate crime. According to their information, Jason acted alone.

Agent Trenton was called down by the arresting officer, Agent Redding. He found out some interesting information about Jason that he thought Agent Trenton should know. He did a background check on Jason, that's when he stumbled onto his brother, Darius 'D-Boy' Jensen himself. Everyone in FBI's New York office knew that Agent Trenton had a hard-on for D-Boy, so he'd definitely want to know this bit of info. If only to rub it in D-Boy's face to taunt him.

Agent Redding hadn't seen Agent Trenton since the Mendez Cartel arrest five years ago. That's how they became good friends. The FBI are like any other fraternity, they stick together and look out for one another.

"It's been a long time since we've hung out! We have to get together after work for a beer one day," Agent Redding said while shaking Agent Trenton's hand.

"I've been so busy with this D-Boy case. I haven't had time for anything else. What you got for me?" Agent Trenton loved new Intel.

"I know you want this guy, D-Boy bad, 'cause of what happened with Steph, God bless the dead. I came across a guy that I have to arrest today that is your guy D-Boy's only sibling, his older brother. He goes by the name DJ Jay-Roc. He's a DJ up at that Hip Hop radio station Hot 104. Between me and you, I fucking hate that jungle music, but to each his own," Agent Redding said.

"What did he do?"

"The charge is called CRIMINAL ENTERPRISE OF FEDERAL PROPERTY. He took money from artists in exchange for radio play. It's like stealing from the Federal government because we own the radio airwaves. Can you believe that? The Feds own the air, that's so funny!"

Agent Trenton started thinking of a way to tie D-Boy into this racket. It was too sudden. He knew he had to take some time putting the puzzle together. It was something for him to look forward to. Anything that would put D-Boy away was worth its weight in gold to Agent Trenton.

"Do you mind if I tag along with you on this arrest?" Agent Trenton asked.

"I wouldn't have it any other way. Let's go." The officers headed for their vehicles.

HOT 104 RADIO STATION

"You're a week behind. You owe me $50k. I need all mine." Jazzy was in a bad mood lately.

"Damn, ma! Why you got to be so rude?" DJ T-1 reached into his money drawer. "Here is $50k. Now don't I always keep it one hundred with you?" He smiled but she didn't respond. She just looked at him with disgust.

"I think I'm pregnant!" Jazzy burst out. "I know it's your baby because I don't think my man can have babies. I'm fertile, so I know it's not me. I fuck with you one time and I get pregnant!" Jazzy started crying.

"Hold on, ma, I didn't cum in you. You better have your man checked out. Sometimes niggas be stressed and they soldiers don't swim hard enough." DJ T-1 was suddenly nervous.

"I'm going to take care of it, don't worry." Jazzy got up to leave.

"That don't mean we can't still mess around. I'll wear a condom next time, okay?"

Jazzy just walked out without responding. *I'm never fucking with you again!* She exited his office.

As she headed toward the DJ booth, she saw six men with big yellow FBI letters written on the back of their jackets heading in the same direction. Her stomach turned, and then her heart beat out of control when they knocked on the door. Jason was doing a live show, so he couldn't stop abruptly.

"Mr. Jason Jensen, please come out with your hands up!" They banged on the door as they yelled his name.

Everyone at Hot 104 stood watching the scene unfold. Everyone knew what those big yellow letters meant, especially Jazzy.

"Please don't arrest him!" Jazzy begged. "He didn't do anything!"

"Miss, please move out of the way. You're interfering with a Federal investigation. Step aside now!" Agent Redding demanded.

She had no choice. Jazzy moved out of their way so they could do their job. She knew exactly why they were arresting her man. She knew it was all her fault for taking DJ T-1 up on his offer. Jazzy wanted to scream at the top of her lungs from frustration.

ALAH ADAMS

"Mr. Jensen! Come out of there in five seconds, or we'll bust the door down!"

What the fuck is going on! Jason thought in a panic. *Why are they locking me up? I didn't do anything.*

"Okay, I'm coming out with my hands up!" he said before exiting the booth.

"Jason Jensen, you're under arrest by the Federal Government of the United States of America. You've been charged with five counts of CRIMINAL ENTERPRISE OF FEDERAL PROPERTY. YOU HAVE THE RIGHT TO REMAIN SILENT. YOU HAVE THE RIGHT TO AN ATTORNEY . . .

Jason was so confused that the words the agent spoke may as well have been French. He thought this was some kind of joke until the cuffs went around his wrists.

The whole staff was watching, especially DJ T-1. Jason looked at Jazzy, who was crying in a corner and looking distraught. The rest of the Hot 104 staff just shook their heads in disbelief. Tracy came out to confront the officer.

"Excuse me, I'm the Program Director of the station. Can you explain what's going on?" Tracy asked in a professional tone.

"We can't discuss anything with you because this is an on-going investigation," Agent Redding replied.

Damn, they got him. Oh well, he has no idea who to tell on so I'm safe, DJ T-1 thought.

* * * * *

D-Boy pulled up to the station at the same time as the FBI agents were entering the Hot 104 building. "I wonder why they're here." D-Boy asked himself as he got out of his vehicle to enter the building as well.

He didn't want to waste any time, and he decided to show his brother the video of Jazzy immediately. He thought, *Why wait and let her continue to deceive Jason? May as well get it over with now. There's no time like the present.*

While he watched the FBI Agents swarm the building, he noticed Agent Trenton leading the pack with another officer. That's when D-Boy pulled back and peeped the scene from a distance. He didn't want to have a run-in with Agent Trenton, but he wanted to know exactly what was going on.

D-Boy got on the elevator behind the agents. They didn't see him when he got off. He made sure he was not in Agent Trenton's view as he watched them. They headed straight for DJ Jay-Roc's booth and asked for him by name.

"Why the fuck are they arresting my brother?" he asked.

He watched the whole episode unfold. He saw Jazzy crying and DJ T-1 looking on from a distance. D-Boy knew that both Jazzy and DJ T-1 were abreast to everything going on. They knew exactly why the Feds were arresting Jason. Neither of them stepped up on his behalf to stop it. They left Jason for dead.

"What did I do? I didn't do nothing! I'm innocent!" Jason yelled as they escorted him to the elevator in cuffs.

D-Boy pretended to be drinking water from a water-fountain when the agents passed him with Jason in tow. That's all D-Boy needed was to run into Agent

135

Trenton while they were arresting his brother. It only would've made the situation worse for Jason.

"Don't worry, big brother, D-Boy got you. They're not getting away with this." D-Boy called up John Gillespie.

"What's up, John? I need that favor you owe me."

"No problem, D-Boy. What can I do for you?" D-Boy was one of John's highest paying clients, so it was always a pleasure to hear from him.

"This time it's not for me, it's for my big brother, Jason. He's been set up to take the fall for taking money to play records, which is a serious federal offense."

"I'm familiar with these types of cases. They're really hard to beat because they have to have you red-handed to arrest you," John replied.

"I have a video of the true culprits exchanging money and talking about the songs."

"Well, say no more. I'll get your brother out by tomorrow. He'll be eating lunch with you at some fancy restaurant." John spoke with confidence.

"Thanks, John," D-Boy replied sincerely.

"Don't mention it. I'll see you tomorrow at court. And bring that video to my office today so I can see it."

"I got you. See you in about an hour." D-Boy hung up the phone.

D-Boy watched them take Jason to jail, something he tried hard to stay away from. Jason prided himself on being a straight and narrow guy. Now he was in cuffs because of his fiancée. D-Boy would've never imagined that his big brother would be in a jail cell, and neither had Jason.

Fortunately for you, your little brother is going to take care of this situation. You won't be doing no jail time, not if I have anything to do about it, D-Boy reflected as he drove toward John's office.

DJ T-1'S OFFICE AT HOT 104 RADIO STATION

"What're we going to do?" Jazzy lost her composure. "They're going to connect the dots in no time."

"Wait a minute, you didn't tell your man that you were collecting $25k a week?" DJ T-1 was about to panic himself. "When they question him he's going to say you gave him those songs to play, then you're going to point to me!"

"Calm down, we have to keep a level head or we're going to go crazy. Let's just think for a minute." Jazzy had other intentions. She was going to look out for her man and herself. As far as she was concerned, DJ T-1 was already thrown under the bus.

"What do you think Jason is going to say to them when they question him? You think he'll just hold the charge down? Or is he the type to tell on his own girl?" DJ T-1 sounded like a man with twenty-four hours to live.

"Well, I know once D-Boy finds out that Jason is in jail he's going to get him out ASAP," Jazzy said with confidence.

"Hold on. Did you say D-Boy was going to get him out? Why would D-Boy get him out?" DJ T-1 asked curiously.

"D-Boy is Jason's little brother." Jazzy said it like it was common knowledge until she realized it wasn't.

"Wait a minute . . . you're telling me that D-Boy is Jason's little brother?" DJ T-1 went silent and thoughts flashed through his mind as if they were racing one another. He was having epiphany after epiphany. Images flashed through his mind from his past, a seedy past full of lies, deceit, and robbery.

He has a brother . . . I thought he was the only son. I didn't shoot Jason when he was a kid. I shot D-Boy, DJ T-1 thought. *That's why I kept looking at him as if I knew him from somewhere, because we saw each other that day when I mistakenly shot him. He had to be no older than nine when it happened.*

"Are you okay?" Jazzy watched DJ T-1 as he went back in time. "Care to share?"

"There's something I have to tell you. I didn't just pick Jason out of thin air to be the new DJ for the show. I picked Jason for a reason. Years ago, Jason's father, OG Jesse, took someone away from me, someone very close to me. It was a botched robbery, and his father killed my only sibling, my little brother Jeffrey Wilshire. He died at twenty-three years old. It was my fault because Jeffery was following me. He did whatever I told him to do. It was my idea to rob OG Jesse. Because he killed my brother, I was going to use his only son as a scapegoat to get this money. I just found out from this conversation that OG Jesse had two sons. I mistakenly shot one of them the day he killed my brother.

"I went by the name Tone back then. After I was shot and my brother died, I became DJ T-1. T-1 is short for Tone, get it? The letter T plus the number one, T-one. Being DJ T-1 saved me from the streets and gave me a legal alternative to make money. I was used to making drug money, so the DJ money was short, until I found out how to hustle artists for money. I've been doing this shit for years. I knew they were investigating me, that's why I created the show. I just couldn't stop getting that money. I'd already become accustomed to living a certain lifestyle. I got greedy, and I knew it was going to come to an ugly end, because I'm addicted. I'm addicted to fast money, I'm addicted to hustling." DJ T-1 was putting everything on the table because he needed to. He'd been holding on to this baggage for so long, he just needed to unload it on someone else for once.

"Wow! I remember the story of D-Boy getting shot when he was nine. Jason would always tell me that D-Boy didn't care if he lived or died after being shot. That was the moment that he decided he was going to be a gangster, and he was going to live life like an outlaw. It's crazy because it did the opposite to Jason. Jason didn't want anything to do with the streets or that gangster life. For us to cross paths like this is crazy, because that one act has deeply affected all of our lives. It murdered your only brother, while tragically wounding a nine-year-old child, and at the same time motivating Jason and yourself to go straight after that one event in history." Jazzy had the ability to speak like a wise sage at times.

Jazzy opened her purse and looked at the money. She almost wanted to throw up just seeing it. She knew the money was the root of her poor decision making. It was the money that made her have sex with DJ T-1. She became disgusted with herself, and she wanted to scream. Yet, she just stared at the $50K in her purse.

"I have to get out of here." She ran out of his office as fast as she could.

"Jazzy! Wait!" It was too late. She was already on the elevator.

She ran to the parking garage and jumped in her car and drove as fast as she could all the way to Long Island, where she and Jason shared an apartment. Jazzy ran up the stairs and packed as many clothes as she could. Then she opened a drawer and removed $100,000 in cash from underneath the folded clothes. She threw it in her purse with the $50k she already had and took in a remorseful deep breath. Set on leaving the mess she'd made behind, she dragged the luggage to the car and drove straight toward JFK airport. At a long red light she went online and bought a ticket on the next flight to Los Angeles, California. She got lucky and found a ticket for 6:00 p.m., which was only a three-hour wait.

"I'm out of here and I'm never looking back." Those were Jazzy's last words before she boarded her plane headed for sunny California.

* * * * *

"So she just skipped town?" Sam asked Jason as he ate jerk chicken.

"Yeah, she couldn't take the shame." Jason answered.

"Will you be having any dessert today, sir?" the waitress asked.

"I'll have my usual red velvet cake." Jason always got the same meal when he came there.

"I'll just have what he's having," Sam said.

"I have to warn you, their red velvet cake is to die for," Jason said jokingly.

"It's your treat, so when in Rome, do as the Romans do."

"Okay."

"That'll be out in a minute," the waitress informed them.

"We have nothing but time," Jason responded.

CHAPTER 14

**Next day in Judge Borelli's Chambers
Eastern District Federal Court Building
Brooklyn, New York**

Your honor, I've never witnessed a case anything like this in my entire career. The arresting officers should've known this was a set-up from the fact that the made up account had the defendant's business name on it. When you add the video to the equation, there is strong enough grounds for immediate dismissal," John said with utmost cockiness.

"We have no problem with that, your honor. In fact, an arrest warrant for a Mr. Anthony 'DJ T-1' Wilshire is being made out as we speak. We have enough evidence to close this case quickly. Mr. Wilshire would be a fool to fight against himself on the video saying he collected the money *"for your little boyfriend to play records."* Yeah, we have enough." The Federal prosecutor replied. "There is the issue of the identity of the young lady that took the money on the video. If Mr. Jensen wants to incriminate her, he can. It'd be nice, but we have enough to indict Mr.

Wilshire." Because Jazzy had her back to the camera, you never saw her face. She was safe.

"Case dismissed! Bailiff, release the defendant," Judge Borelli ordered.

The bailiff sent the message. "Release Jason Jensen."

D-Boy was waiting in the lobby for his brother to be released. When Jason came out, D-Boy was the only person there for him. He knew for sure that Jazzy was going to be there too. Jason didn't get the memo yet, but he would.

"Where's Jazzy?" Jason asked in a confused tone.

"She's gone, Jason. Jazzy skipped town. I went by your apartment, and she was in such a rush that she left the door wide open. I went in and saw all her stuff missing out of the drawers, so I assumed she left." D-Boy saw the confusion on his face.

"Why would she leave? I mean, I need her now more than ever." Jason couldn't fathom what was going on. "This shit is crazy, D-Boy. First I get arrested for some shit I didn't do. They're accusing me of collecting money to play records. I know that's a felony, and I would never do that. How does this happen to me?"

"Let's get out of here. This place gives me the creeps," D-Boy said.

As they walked to the car, D-Boy was thinking of a way to break the bad news about Jazzy. This was the hardest thing he had to tell his brother. He knew how Jason felt about her. For Jazzy, he was ready to go against everyone, even his only brother.

"There's something I have to show you, Jason."
D-Boy pulled up the footage of Jazzy sitting in DJ T-1's office. He saw DJ T-1 give her $25,000 to play the records. Jason didn't speak, his face just kept contorting. Then when it got to the part where DJ T-1 was having sex with Jazzy. He couldn't take it.

"No! That's not Jazzy! Turn it off. I don't want to see anymore!" His eyes welled up with giant tears. "Tell me that isn't my Jazzy, D-Boy! Tell me it isn't her!" D-Boy hugged him as tight as he could.

"It's going to be okay, big bro. Be strong." D-Boy had never seen Jason break down like this.

"How could she do this to me? I was so good to that woman, and this is what I get!" His pain was turning into rage. "I should've listened to you when you told me she was sneaky. I can't believe this is happening!"

"It's not the end of the world. The case got dismissed and you can probably get your job back at Hot 104. Once they learn the truth that DJ T-1 was the one breaking the law, they're going to need you. Plus you're the best DJ they got!" D-Boy tried to lift his spirits.

Jason was silent. All he could think about was Jazzy. Her betrayal hit him like a freight train, out of nowhere. He would never imagine Jazzy doing any of this behind his back. He wanted to break down and cry like a baby, but he didn't. Jason stayed strong in front of D-Boy. He didn't want to show any more weakness.

"You're right, D-Boy. I can come back from this. I can run things at Hot 104, and I have the number one show on the radio in that time slot. I'm about to turn up!"

"That's what I'm talking about! Turn up, big bro. You don't need that 'ho! Like you say on your show, Let's get it!" D-Boy's tone genuinely uplifted Jason.

"Word! I'm about to take this DJ shit to another level!" Something was happening to Jason. This situation had turned him into a beast! "I want you to be my manager from now on. I want to take all those artists that paid to get their music played and put their music on my debut album!"

"Now you're thinking! That's a brilliant idea, Jay. You can drop Shoota's new song as the first single from your album. You work at the station, so you can blast off all the music from your album. We'll be unstoppable!"

Jason saw the vision clearly. This was the opportunity of a lifetime. "You're right, D-Boy. I can legally play records on my own without breaking the law. We might be on to something, D-Boy."

"We might be? My nigga, we *are* on to something!" D-Boy was never this excited. "Let's go to the studio and get all the music on one disc, then you can put your signature drops throughout the album. There you have it, the new DJ Jay-Roc album!"

"This is going to work, little brother. Let's get it!" Jason almost forgot about Jazzy.

"What're you going to call the album?" D-Boy asked.

He had to think a minute. "Because this whole idea came from me getting arrested and seeing Jazzy for what she really is. I'm going to call it, *The Awakening!*"

"That's a good concept. I feel real good about this. You always wanted me to get out of the game. This might be my way out. It goes back to what Grandpa Joe used to say: *Sometimes you got to get knocked down to come up.* If you wouldn't have gotten knocked down by Jazzy and DJ T-1, you wouldn't have come up with that brilliant idea to drop a DJ Jay-Roc album." D-Boy spoke with wisdom.

"You right, little brother," Jason replied.

They drove toward the Music Palace studio, ready to get to work. Jazzy's betrayal lightly danced on the edges of his mind, torturing Jason's thoughts. Images of him choking her unconscious while music from his new album played, flooded his head.

HOT 104 RADIO STATION

"It's your boy DJ T-1 filling in for DJ Jay-Roc. I got some listening treats for your ears, so stay tuned!" DJ T-1 sounded like a nervous wreck, but the show had to go on.

"He sounds terrible!" Tracy noticed. "He thinks he's in the clear. I know he had something to do with DJ Jay-Roc's arrest," Tracy said to Thomas.

"The Hot Spot at Two is our highest rated show. We can't stop it now!" Thomas was the general manager, so everything fell on his shoulders.

As if on cue, the FBI entered Hot 104 for the second time in two days. "We have an arrest warrant for a Mr. Anthony 'DJ T-1' Wilshire," Agent Redding announced.

"There goes the show. Lucky for us the show is over in five minutes, so the audience isn't going to notice it. What about tomorrow?" Tracy said.

"Damn! We have to figure something out fast!" Thomas panicked.

Like a bad repeat, the FBI took DJ T-1 from the same booth they took Jason from a day before. "You're under arrest for five counts of Criminal Enterprise of Federal Property, and two counts of Identity Fraud. Please place your hands behind your back. You have the right to remain silent, anything you say can and will be held against you . . ." They escorted him from the building as they read him the rest of his rights.

"What's the status of DJ Jay-Roc?" Thomas asked.

"He'll be out on bail today, hopefully. I have his cell phone listed. I'll give him a call to see if he's available," Tracy responded.

Tracy opened up the company contacts and found Jason's number. He didn't answer the phone, but returned the missed call a few minutes later.

"Hello? Did someone just call DJ Jay-Roc?" Jason asked.

"Yes! I did, you're home!" Tracy was ecstatic. "The FBI just came in here and arrested DJ T-1 like five minutes ago. Jason, we need you at the station. By the way, what's the status of your case?"

"My case was dismissed on account of DJ T-1 setting me up. He left a video of him giving my

fiancée—I mean my ex—money to play records. Then
he fucked her in his office." Jason was in the studio
with D-Boy and Shoota when Tracy called.

"Wow! Are you serious? There's a video?
Anyway, none of that matters. Will you be available to
work tomorrow?" Tracy sounded desperate.

"Of course I'll be available to work tomorrow.
And I have a surprise for Hot 104. I'm dropping an
album. I'm going to turn up!" He was in rare form,
getting burnt by Jazzy changed Jason for the better. No
more Mr. Nice Guy.

"That sounds incredible, Jason! I'm going to tell
Thomas all about it. I can't wait to see you tomorrow. I
mean ummm . . . I'll see you tomorrow," Tracy said,
hanging up the phone and grinning wide. "Maybe I
will get what I want," she said as she looked out the
window at the beautiful NYC skyline from the forty-
eighth floor.

* * * * *

"Dessert's finally here!" Sam said, intruding on
Jason's memory.

The red velvet cake was brought out. Jason took
his time, but Sam dug in immediately. "You were
right. This red velvet cake is to die for."

"It's one of my favorite Jamaican dishes."

"It sounds like Tracy may be your favorite dish.
So . . . you started banging this chick, Tracy, huh?"
Sam chuckled.

"Something like that—but let me finish telling you
the story before I get side-tracked."

148

CHAPTER 15

D-BOY'S HOUSE
Jamaica Estates

D-Boy was watching the 10 o'clock news when they showed DJ T-1's mug shot. "A popular DJ at the world famous Hip Hop radio station Hot 104 was arrested today. Forty-two-year-old Anthony 'DJ T-1' Wilshire was charged with five counts of Criminal Enterprise of Federal Property, and two counts of identity fraud. This comes just one day after the arrest of another poplar DJ at Hot 104, DJ Jay-Roc for similar charges. Sources tell us that DJ Jay-Roc was exonerated, and his charges were dismissed in Federal court earlier today." The anchorman went on to talk about more news, but he said a name that caught D-Boy's attention.

Anthony Wilshire, where do I know that name from? D-Boy asked. *Wilshire, that's the last name of the guy that shot me. I wonder if there's any connection.*

D-Boy kept a photo album with old newspaper clippings of his and his family's criminal history. He had clippings that went back to Grandpa Joe's time when he got caught for robbing a bank in the 60s. Also, he had clippings of his first arrest that made the paper when they named him 'The Baby Faced Gangster.' He was looking for one clipping in particular, the one about that fateful day, the day he was shot.

He found it and started reading it. He tried to stay away from the memory of that day because he was so young. D-Boy had grown into this tough gangster, but he was once a scared little boy on the day he was shot. Darius Jensen was an innocent child looking for his father when he was gunned down in his own home. Reading the article brought back images and memories he'd long buried. This was an unearthing.

Darius Jensen, a nine-year-old boy was shot in his chest yesterday in a botched robbery attempt. His father, thirty-two-year-old Jesse OG Jensen was arrested for the murder of twenty-three-year-old Jeffrey Wilshire, whom Jesse claimed shot his nine-year-old son.

"That's what I was looking for! I knew it was something about that name that was familiar. I wonder if he's related to Jeffrey Wilshire. It can't be a coincidence." His intuition was tingling. "There's only one person that I can ask. Only problem with that is I have to travel all the way to Attica to talk to my father." D-Boy contemplated. "I'll get to that later. Let me check my iTunes account."

Shoota's song was selling units every day. He sold a total of 126,778 units of his single "New John Gotti" in six weeks. At .99 cents per download, and after deducting iTunes fee for their services, the artist gets .55 cents per unit. It all added up to $69,727.90, which wasn't bad considering they only invested $20,000 total.

"Easy money, no hassle with the police and rival crews. I think I can learn to like this music business." D-Boy thought of ways to expand. "Once we drop the next two singles, our account should triple!" His thoughts were interrupted by his cell phone ringing. The caller ID revealed his big brother Jason was calling.

"What're you doing?" Jason asked.

"Planning my next attack, why?"

"Come down to the station. I want to talk to you about something."

"Why can't you just talk on the phone? I got some business to take care of." D-Boy wasn't fronting, he was about to go collect money on what he liked to call, *The Money Route*.

"Okay, I wanted to say this to you face to face, but since you insist, I'll tell you over the phone." He paused to collect his composure. "I want to apologize for standing up for Jazzy when she snapped at you that day. When I think about it, I was dead wrong. She had no right to talk to you like that. All you asked was if you could speak to me alone, and she snapped. The only reason she did that was because she knew she was living foul, so she was taking it out on you. She was the one getting money on the side, among other things. But I'm getting over that part of my life and moving on." Talking about it hurt a bit, but day by day Jason was healing.

"I accept your apology because I love you, because you're my only brother, and I know you're a good dude. I knew Jazzy had the wool pulled over your eyes. It was only a matter of time before she revealed her true colors." D-Boy was happy that Jason was getting better. He thought it would take him years to get over Jazzy, his first adult love.

"I'm not going to front, there's another reason I'm feeling better today. When I came to work, Tracy gave me a tight hug and a kiss that told me she wants the kid. She always threw me signals, but Jazzy was always there cock-blocking. Now that Jazzy is out of the picture, I think Tracy is a choice pick." Jason smiled.

"That's what the fuck I'm talking about, my nigga! I know who you talking about. She's pretty and smart, and not for nothing. She puts Jazzy to shame in every department!" Jason knew D-Boy was exaggerating, but it was boosting his confidence.

"You know what? You're right. I'm going to do my thing for once. I'm always holding back trying to be this perfect guy that doesn't get into trouble and look where that got me. I'm not saying I'm going to go buck wild like you. I'm just going to live my life with more ambition. I have to stop being so timid and go after what I want in life." Jason knew that Tracy was within earshot of his conversation. "Let me call you later. I got to go."

Damn Tracy! You are beautiful. Why didn't I notice you like this before? Jason thought as he turned to face her.

"What's up, Tracy? I just wanted to thank you for giving me my job back." Jason needed to break the ice.

AMERICAN D - BOY

"You're welcome, Jason. You are one of the best DJs in NYC, so we had to give you another chance. Besides, I knew that you didn't do what they accused you of. I told Thomas that yesterday. You just started working here. How could you possibly put together something so elaborate? I knew it was DJ T-1."

"Good thing you spoke on my behalf, or I wouldn't have a job. What are you doing after work?"

"Nothing."

"Would you like to go to dinner with me?" Jason was still shy, but this was a start.

"Is this a date?" Tracy asked, showing her pearly white teeth.

"I guess so. Yes, it's a date." He smiled back.

"Okay, I'll meet you downstairs at 4:30." Tracy walked away knowing that he would view her ample backside.

"Damn! She has a nice ass!" Jason was feeling like a new man, just thinking about being with Tracy.

That was until he was brought back down to earth with a phone call. This wasn't just any phone call, it was Jazzy. He closed his eyes and took a deep breath. "Should I even answer?" Jason wondered. "Fuck it, I have to face her sooner or later. No time like the present. Hello."

"Hi Jason." Jazzy's tone was very solemn. "I know you got out because I saw it on the Internet. How are you?"

"I'm good. What about you?" Jason held back his emotions.

"Not so good."

"Jazzy, how could you do this to me, to us? I loved you so much and you stabbed me in the heart!" He couldn't contain it.

"What do you mean, baby? I would never do anything to hurt you." Jazzy mocked sincerity.

"I saw the video of you and DJ T-1 breaking money in half and of you having sex with him in his office. How could you do this to me?" He needed to hear anything, an excuse even. Just something to give him closure.

"What're you talking about? What video?"

"Oh, you don't know. Well, when you were in DJ T-1's office collecting money and getting fucked over the desk, he was filming all of it." Jason went silent to let it sink in. "That's how my case got dismissed, and don't worry, I didn't snitch on you and tell them who the girl in the video was. They couldn't make out your face because your back was to the camera."

Jazzy couldn't believe what he'd just said. It was almost like she didn't hear him, but she did and she was in a state of denial.

"You're bugging, right? There's no video of me and DJ T-1. It can't be!" She couldn't imagine there being a video of her and DJ T-1. "You saw this video?"

"Yes, I saw the video, so there's no need denying it! You know what you did!" Jason was furious now.

"I'm sorry, Jason. I'm so sorry. Please forgive me!" Jazzy wanted to die right there. The pain was excruciating. "We can get past this. I can be the girl you fell in love with. Please give me another chance, I'm begging you."

Jason almost entertained the thought until Tracy walked past him and winked her eye. "No, I don't think that's a good idea right now. You hurt me deep, Jazzy. It'll never be the same between us."

"Please give me another chance. I promise I'll never lie to you again." Jazzy was determined to win him back.

"You have to give me time to even consider taking you back. For now I think it's best for us to be apart."

"I understand. I called for a few reasons. One was to see that you're all right. The second reason was to warn you about something." Jazzy paused before speaking. "DJ T-1 is Tone from back in the day. The same Tone that shot D-Boy when he was nine. He chose you for the DJ job because he said OG killed his brother."

"That's impossible. My dad killed the man that shot D-Boy. He's free styling because there was only one guy in that robbery, and he was killed on the scene." Jason had the facts backward, but he didn't know it. OG had to change the real story to get less time.

"I'm just telling you what he told me. He said something about he thought you were the only son. He didn't know that D-Boy was your brother. I'm just telling you what he said, that's the least I can do is to warn you about him." Jazzy was sincere.

"I have to ask my father. He's the only one that would know." He glanced at his watch. It was 3:15, almost time to meet with Tracy. "I have to go now. I guess this is goodbye." Jason didn't know what else to say.

"I guess so. Don't be a stranger." Jazzy spoke with pain in her voice.

"I won't." Jason hung up because he hated long goodbyes.

* * * * *

Jazzy was devastated. She didn't see this one coming. She lay on the bed and wept like a little girl. She felt so sorry for what she did to Jason. Jazzy knew he didn't deserve it. She'd lost everything, her relationship, her respect, all over money.

How could I have been so stupid! I shouldn't have taken the money. I shouldn't have fucked DJ T-1! I shouldn't have betrayed the only man that ever really loved me. I'm going to regret this for the rest of my life, whatever is left of it because I just want to end it now! Jazzy contemplated suicide, staring at the razor blade lying on the bathroom sink. *One swift cut of the veins and it's all over.*

She picked up the razor blade and looked at herself in the mirror, hating her reflection. It reminded her of something dirty and foul. She pressed the blade against her wrist, just enough to puncture her skin. A small trickle of blood dripped from her wrist, and she let it fall into the porcelain white sink. She liked the pattern of red and porcelain making a crimson design in the sink. Jazzy pressed the blade harder, this time cutting into a vein. The blood poured from her wrist like a faucet now.

"Oh shit! There's no turning back now!" Jazzy got frightened at the thought that she was about to really die. She was just contemplating suicide with no real reservations, now it was too late. The blood that nourished the life force energy of her body was leaving its host. She wanted to stop the bleeding, and she tried to close the wound with her free hand, to no avail. The blood had already found an opening and it was leaving her body too fast. It only took minutes before Jazzy had lost enough blood to pass out on the bathroom floor. Her heartbeat was faint—her brain was already shutting down. She had seconds before her life was over. With her last bit of life, she took out her cell phone and typed a text to Jason.

Jason, I know you can't forgive me, that's why I don't want to live. I love you and I'm so sorry. I'll see you on the other side.

Love always,

Jasmine

She pressed the send button.

Her last message was sent to Jason Jensen, her lost love. Jasmine Guillermo died at the age of twenty-five years old from a broken heart.

* * * * *

Jason received the message in a split second. He read it and tried to call her. "Jazzy! Pick up the phone!" He wanted to make sure she was joking because her text was too real.

"What happened? Is everything okay?" Tracy asked.

"I think Jazzy just committed suicide. She sent me this crazy text about how she'll see me on the other side, and she doesn't want to live anymore." Jason was panting at the thought that she might be dead.

"Jason, I need you to calm down and think for a moment. Do you really think she was serious?" Tracy was very concerned. Even though they were enemies, she'd never wish death on Jazzy.

"I don't know . . . She isn't answering the phone. And I don't know where she's at. She skipped town."

"Let's not jump to conclusions. She might've been bluffing." Tracy tried to calm him.

"Damn! I don't know . . ."

"You guys have been together for a while, so ask yourself if she'd ever go through with committing suicide. Is that something she'd ever truly consider?"

No. It was Jason's immediate answer as he contemplated Tracy's words. He and Jazzy were raised in an environment that frowned upon suicide. Their life goals had always been about the hustle and survival. When things got bad, they were taught to hustle that much harder. "You know what? You may be right."

Tracy's comment jump started his brain. Jazzy had always been a bit of a drama queen, and it wouldn't surprise him if she'd come up with this suicide scheme to try to get back with him. "Damn . . . It's just like her to be fronting to get my attention. She's always been good at manipulating me." He shook his head.

"Let's go out to dinner, Tracy." Jason wanted to go out with Tracy more so for the rebound than anything at this point.

"Let's also try to have a good time," Tracy replied.

"At this point I need to have a good time. Let's go."

In a matter of hours, Tracy and Jason clicked like a combination lock. They had the time of their lives! They couldn't stop talking. This was the most that

Jason told a woman about himself. He felt open and honest with Tracy. He was comfortable being himself. He hadn't opened up this much with Jazzy in the beginning. Maybe the connection wasn't as strong as his connection with Tracy.

She was feeling the same, and she'd never told a man this much about herself on the first date. There was an innocence that allowed Tracy to be herself as well. They were alike in so many ways that she knew this was a love connection moment. Tracy was no novice when it came to men. She learned to trust her gut. Her gut was telling her that Jason was the right man for her!

"It seems like I've known you all of my life. I really enjoyed your company, Tracy. You made me forget about all the drama that's been going on in my life the last couple of days," Jason said.

"I'm glad I could be of service. I've told you things tonight that I haven't told anyone. That's weird, because I'm usually very guarded." Tracy knew where this was leading.

"Well, I guess this is good night." Jason kissed Tracy on the cheek. "Thank you for coming out. I really appreciate it."

"Anytime, in fact I was thinking about doing this again tomorrow if you're free," Tracy asked.

"I wouldn't miss it for the world. So tomorrow it's a date?"

It's a date." Tracy smiled. "Good night, Jason." Tracy walked to her brownstone door, opened it and turned to see if Jason was still there. Just like the gentleman Tracy knew he was, Jason was still in his car waiting to see that she made it in the house safe and sound.

Tracy blew him a kiss before entering her brownstone.

As he drove off Jason thought, *I really hope I was right about Jazzy just trying to get my attention. I can't see her actually killing herself. She wouldn't do anything crazy like that. Would she?*

AMERICAN D - BOY

CHAPTER 16

CORONER'S OFFICE
Los Angeles, California

Two days later, Jazzy was found dead at the Beverly Hills Hilton on the bathroom floor by housekeeping. The front desk noticed she wasn't responding to calls from room service so they sent someone to see if everything was okay. It didn't take long before the LAPD HOMICIDE was on the scene investigating. Didn't need much detective work to figure out that she killed herself, so she was quickly taken to the coroner.

"She had identification on her. It says she's a Miss Jasmine Guillermo from Brooklyn, New York," homicide detective Rawlings said to the coroner.

"She's a long way from home. We need to notify her next of kin about her death. We're ruling this one as a suicide. There's no evidence to indicate otherwise. Oh, and she was five weeks pregnant," the coroner replied.

"Damn, she didn't just take her own life, she took the child's life too." Detective Rawlings shook his head in disappointment.

161

The coroner slid Jasmine's body into its slot in the wall. Detective Rawlings noticed that she had her cell phone in her hand when they found her body. A hunch told him that he could find out whom she last communicated with. It didn't take a genius to figure out that Jason was the last person to talk to Jazzy. The text was consistent with the official time of death.

Detective Rawlings dialed the number he got from Jazzy's phone.

Jason answered on the third ring.

"Hello? This is homicide detective Arthur Rawlings from the Los Angeles homicide division. Do you know Jasmine Guillermo?"

"Yes I do. She's my ex." Jason braced himself. "She was my girlfriend. Why? What happened to her?" He was already in panic mode.

"I'm not supposed to do this, but she committed suicide two days ago."

Jason was stunned. He heard what Detective Rawlings said, but it took time to register.

"Hello?"

"Yeah, I'm still here. I don't know what to say. She texted me two days ago. She said she would see me on the other side, but I thought she was bluffing." Tears were already running down his face.

"I saw that text, that's why I called you." He paused before telling him the rest of this tragic event. "There's one more thing. She was five weeks pregnant according to the coroner. Once again, I'm sorry about your loss." Detective Rawlings hung up the phone.

Jason dropped his body down on the plush couch in his living room. He couldn't stop crying. This news would change his life forever. Jazzy represented his only real experience in love. Before Jazzy, he had non-meaningful flings with women he'd met in the club. Jason made a note to himself never to get serious with a girl he'd met at Club Delight. Jazzy was the exception.

When he met Jazzy there was something about her that attracted him that went beyond the physical. Jason felt Jazzy's vibrant energy—she was a mover and a shaker. They'd met through a mutual friend and hit it off. They became an item in no time. They were in love. Jason could never deny the fact that he was in love with Jazzy. Through it all, even with the cheating and the money, he still loved her. There would always be a spot in his heart for Jazzy.

Jason didn't want to go to work today, but he had to. He just got his job back and he couldn't risk losing it. He forced himself to get dressed, and he miraculously made it to the radio station. Tracy was the first person Jason saw when he entered the building. He couldn't hide his pain, not even with the dark glasses he had on.

"Hey Jason, are you okay?" Tracy noticed his demeanor immediately.

"No, I'm not okay. Jazzy's dead. She committed suicide two days ago while we were out having a great time. She really did it. She really killed herself. And she was pregnant. Who knows if the baby was mine or DJ T-1's?" Jason couldn't hold back the anguish.

Tracy hugged him. "Jason, it'll be okay. She's in a better place."

"I feel like it's my fault!" He was in no shape to work.

"It's not your fault, Jason! You didn't make her do any of those things she did to lose you. You were good to her, and I'm not going to let you blame yourself for this," Tracy said defiantly.

Jason thought about it. "You're right. I just wish she would've been stronger. She was always the rock in our relationship."

"You have to live your life now. She loved you and that's what she would want for you. You have to be the rock in your own life now."

As Tracy was consoling Jason, D-Boy entered the building with Shoota.

"Jason, what's going on?" D-Boy asked, seeing his brother looking distraught.

"She's dead, D-Boy! Jazzy is gone. She committed suicide two days ago in Los Angeles, California." Tears streamed down his face.

D-Boy was heartless, but he felt it when Jason told him the news. He didn't care for Jazzy, but she became like a family member over the years. She made Jason happy, and that's all that really mattered to D-Boy.

"Jazzy was like my first love." Tears clutched his throat as he spoke. "I will always love Jazzy."

D-Boy hugged Jason, "Damn, I'm sorry to hear that. I know you're fucked up, I know it. Just hold your head, big brother, hold your head." D-Boy almost shed a tear, but none actually fell.

Jason almost felt himself faint from the euphoria of what was going on. "I have to sit down."

D-Boy and Shoota grabbed his arms to support him.

"I'm sorry to hear that, Jay-Roc. I know you was with her for a minute. That's messed up, my nigga." Shoota offered his condolence.

"You have to be strong and pull yourself together," D-Boy said in Jason's ear.

"I'm going to be okay." Jason took a deep breath, and that's when he thought about what Jazzy told him about DJ T-1. "Excuse me. D-Boy, I have to talk to you in private."

D-Boy and Jason stepped outside by the lobby.

"Jazzy told me some crazy shit about this dude, DJ T-1 before she killed herself." Jason had to compose himself before speaking. "She said that his real name is Tone, and that he's the one that shot you in your chest when you were nine. He picked me to be the DJ as a scapegoat for his little scam because he thought I was Dad's only son. He said that Dad killed his little brother Jeffrey during the robbery attempt, that's why he wanted revenge."

D-Boy quickly processed the information. "That can't be true, because Daddy told me that he killed the guy that shot me in the chest and that's how he got charged with manslaughter instead of murder."

"That's what I told her, but she said DJ T-1 told her himself. He didn't know you were my brother until the Feds arrested me, that's when she told him we were brothers."

"The only way this could be true is if Dad says it is. He's the only one that would know." D-Boy's intuition was itching.

165

ALAH ADAMS

"That's what I thought when she told me." Jason's senses were tingling also. He felt there may be some truth to it.

"Let's go visit him tomorrow, that's the best way to get to the bottom of it." D-Boy knew Jason didn't like visiting their dad in prison, but this was an exception.

"Okay, I'll go with you tomorrow. I have to get ready for the show. I'll talk to you later." Jason was still feeling the effects of his loss.

"Before you leave, I came here to give you this." D-Boy handed Jason a disc. "This is the master copy of your debut album. Congratulations, DJ Jay-Roc!" D-Boy shook Jason's hand.

"Wow! This made my day. Thank you, D-Boy. I couldn't have done this without you."

"You showed me that I have talents other than hustling drugs. I'm ready to take this music shit to the next level. We got Shoota's and your album. We might as well start a label and put this music out ourselves and make all the money!" D-Boy was never this excited about anything but selling drugs.

"Let's get it!" Jason replied in his signature DJ voice. "I'm about to play this whole album today. Fuck what anybody has to say! This is my shit!"

D-Boy had never seen Jason this amped before. He was like a different person. "That's what I'm talking about! I'ma have to meet with this lawyer to finalize the paperwork to start the label. I'm going to make you and Shoota President and Vice President of the company. Of course, I'm the CEO." D-Boy did a little research before jumping into it.

166

"I'm impressed. It sounds like you know what you're doing. We'll talk about it later." Jason dashed off to do his show.

D-Boy thought about what Jason told him about DJ T-1. *It kind of makes sense for some reason. Why else would he do Jason so greasy? He knew that Jason would go down when they investigated it. He didn't know that Jason was my brother because he wouldn't have asked me to kill Jermaine and get the phone.*

D-Boy saw Shoota coming toward him. "Did you give Jason the CD?" he asked.

"Oh yeah, it's on and popping. You got thirty shows lined up already, and counting! We about to drop this DJ Jay-Roc album at the same time that we drop your album. I believe in doubling up, that's how I always come out on top." D-Boy was enthusiastic about the music business.

"I already have over a million views for that video we posted on Worldstar Hip Hop, and that was yesterday!" Shoota was animated.

"Let's go down to this lawyer's office to start this record label officially! I'm trying to leave all this illegal business behind me. I'm going to make more from the music business in one year, than drugs or any of that shit ever made me." D-Boy was passionate about making the transition.

They drove to downtown Manhattan to the law offices of John Gillespie. On the way there D-Boy thought about the name Jeffrey. *Where do I know that name Jeffrey from? That's the name from the newspaper article, Jeffrey Wilshire. That's the same last name as DJ T-1. Maybe DJ T-1 was telling the truth. Only one way to find out.*

When they arrived at John's office, it was time to name the label and sign the paperwork. D-Boy didn't have a name for the label. He wanted Shoota's and Jason's opinion before he gave it an official name. He just wanted the name to represent something that he was about, something that reflected his lifestyle without being too straightforward.

"Hey, D-Boy, today's your big day. Today, you become a legal business owner. How do you feel?" John asked.

"I'm very excited, but I still don't have a name for the company." D-Boy hated to be indecisive.

"Well, you can't sign the paperwork until you have a name for the company."

"I think you should call it D-Boy Records since you're the CEO," Shoota suggested.

"That's cool, but I think we should put something in front of D-Boy," D-Boy replied.

"I have an idea. Why don't you call it American D-Boy Entertainment? If you call it an entertainment company instead of a record company it encompasses the whole entertainment business and not just music," John pointed out.

"That's it! American D-Boy Entertainment!" D-Boy agreed.

John got all the paperwork together. "Sign here, here, and here." D-Boy signed at the marked places. "Now, Shoota, you sign where it says Vice President." Shoota signed his name on the line. "Your President can come down after the paperwork is submitted. You can add officers anytime you feel like it."

"So that's it? I'm officially a legal business owner?" D-Boy asked.

"Yes sir. I'm going to file the paperwork with the State of New York's Department of State, Division of Corporations and its official. The minute they receive the paperwork, American D-Boy Entertainment exists," John replied.

"Let's go celebrate!" D-Boy was elated.

"Word! I'm a Vice President. I can't believe it!" Shoota said.

"Let's go to Club Delight tonight, Jason's old stomping grounds. First, let's go back to Hot 104 to tell Jason the good news," D-Boy said.

* * * * *

They went back to Hot 104 and waited for Jason's show to end. They told him about the news, and he was just as excited as they were. Later that night, they all went down to Club Delight to celebrate the start of American D-Boy Entertainment.

When they arrived, the owner Jack was about to tell the security not to let D-Boy in. D-Boy saw the move before it happened, and he decided to try something different.

"What's up, Jack? Let me talk to you for a minute," D-Boy said, pulling him aside. "I know we've had some differences. I want to apologize to you for the way I acted in the past. I've turned a new leaf, and I'm no longer involved with illegal activities, and in

ALAH ADAMS

fact, we're here to celebrate the start of my first legit company, American D-Boy."

Jack was impressed by D-Boy's new demeanor. "Congratulations, D-Boy, I'm very proud of you. Come on in and celebrate, first bottle is on me," Jack replied sincerely.

They got the party started by offering all the ladies free drinks. That got all the beautiful women to come over to their VIP section. They had their own party going on in their section. They didn't even notice the haters on the sideline watching. The Haitians that D-Boy had beef with were in the building, and they were scoping D-Boy's every move.

"To American D-Boy Entertainment!" D-Boy raised his glass in the air for a toast.

"To American D-Boy Entertainment!" everyone shouted in unison.

"American D-Boy Entertainment. So that's what he's been up to. He's been falling back from the game lately. But that's not going to keep us off his ass. He killed my brother, and I want D-Boy dead even if it's the last thing I do." Andrew was the brother of Amos, the Haitian kingpin that Shoota killed for D-Boy.

D-Boy was having the time of his life. Finally, he was feeling free from the life of crime that gripped his existence. He wanted out, but it wasn't going to be that easy for him. D-Boy made so many enemies that he would have to move to a different country to avoid all the beef. Even then he would still be hunted by the FBI, so there was nowhere to hide because their jurisdiction was worldwide. D-Boy was a highly wanted man.

170

AMERICAN D-BOY

"D-Boy! D-Boy! D-Boy!" they shouted, waiting for the man of the hour to give a few words.

"It's been a long journey for me to get to where I am today. I was shot in my chest at nine years old, and there's been countless attempts on my life since then. I want to live. I'm not trying to die out here in these streets over some money. I'm making an announcement. As of today, I'm throwing in the towel. I'm done with hustling in the streets. The only hustling I'm doing from now on is in the music business." The crowd cheered. D-Boy's words were inspirational to all that knew him, except for Amos's brother, Andrew.

"I'm still going to murder you. You think you're going to kill my brother and it's okay!" Andrew spoke to his two cohorts as if they were his brother. "I don't give a fuck about his American D-Boy bullshit!"

"I'm very proud of you, D-Boy. This is a major move for you. You've been a street dude for your whole life. This is big! I'm riding with you all the way, little brother." Jason toasted with D-Boy.

"That means a lot to me coming from you. You made it out the hood the right way. I've always been proud of you, because you come from the same place I come from. Our whole family is hustlers, going all the way back to slavery, but you made it out. I'm tired of being shot at, and shooting people. The FBI, DEA, ATF, and the NYPD investigating me, trying to put me away for life! And all for what? A little bit of money? Some so-called street credibility?" D-Boy was in rare form. "You know what made me say fuck the game? First when they killed Steph." He paused because that wound was still raw. "When I talked to those FBI agents, I realized that I can't win. If I don't get out the game, I'm going to end up in prison for the rest of my life, or dead. I don't have any children, no wife, nothing but some dirty money that I can't even spend more than $10,000 at a time, or the Feds are coming for me. That day I told myself, I don't want to do this shit anymore! Sometimes you get tired, Jay. I'm just tired."

Jason had never witnessed his little brother speaking like this. He felt sorry and joy at the same time. He was sorry that they both had to endure so much negativity. From birth they were around drugs and criminal activity. They had no choice in the matter. Things may've been different if they had other parents.

Jason was still mourning the loss of Jazzy. Though he tried to hide it, the damage was deep. At the same time he was jubilant that D-Boy was making the transition before it was too late. Jason feared for D-Boy's life every day. He knew D-Boy had beef with some dangerous men. It was torturous on his soul to think that any day his only sibling would be murdered in the streets.

"This is definitely a reason to celebrate, little brother." Jason stood on the posh sofa. "We're about to take over the rap game! It's your boy DJ Jay-Roc in the motherfucking building! Get used to the name, American D-Boy!" He spoke in his signature DJ voice. "Repeat after me— American D-Boy!"

"American D-Boy!" a sea of voices shouted back.

"American D-Boy!" Jason repeated.

"American D-Boy!" the crowd chanted and D-Boy smiled.

AMERICAN D - BOY

*****

Sam finished up the red velvet cake as if it was his last meal, savoring every bite. "Hold on, I don't get it. D-Boy got out of the game and started a legitimate company. So why did he end up still getting killed?" Sam asked as if fishing for information.

"No one really knows who killed D-Boy. It could've been the Haitians, or the FBI." Jason paused. "It could've even been George and his people because they weren't going to let him get out of the game alive." Jason often stared into outer space when thinking deeply.

Sam looked behind him. "Is there something wrong? You were just in the Twilight Zone."

"I was just thinking, whoever killed my brother is still out there. Who knows if he's not finished?"

"You have a point."

"I'm not the same punk ass kid that's scared of guns anymore. After all this drama, I got a gun permit and copped me a few guns for my own protection." Jason lifted his shirt. "I'm strapped right now, and I've been going to the gun range practicing my aim."

"I don't blame you, kid."

"You know what's crazy? As I'm telling you this story it's giving me ideas of who might be responsible for D-Boy's death. When I find out who murdered my brother, I'm going to kill them if it's the last thing I ever do in life." Jason gave Sam a serious look and Sam's eyes wandered as if he was hiding something.

"I feel you, kid. Hell, I might even help you."

"Good looking, Sam." Jason thought that was peculiar for Sam to say he'd help him kill his brother's killer.

"Don't mention it."

I can't put my finger on it, but there's more to Sam than meets the eye, Jason thought.

CHAPTER 17
ATTICA CORRECTIONAL FACILITY
Attica, New York

What's good in the hood?" OG hugged both his sons at the same time with his huge arms.

"How's the radio station treating you? I hear you're a big deal in NYC. All the young cats that come in here off the streets know who you are." OG spoke proudly of Jason.

"It's okay. I'm making the best out of it," Jason replied.

"I heard about your little brush with the law. It was all over the news. I was saying, Jason hates jail. I know he's bugging out." OG knew Jason wasn't built for jail.

"That's the same thing I said, Dad. Jason is probably in there praying to Jesus Christ to get him out of there." D-Boy chimed in on the conversation.

"Enough about me. D-Boy has some good news to tell you." Jason couldn't wait to tell OG.

"This has to be good, because I speak to D-Boy on the regular and he didn't tell me anything."

"I started a legit company called American D-Boy Entertainment yesterday. We're dropping two albums next month, DJ Jay-Roc's album and my first artist, Shoota," D-Boy spoke humbly.

"Congratulations! I'm so proud of you, D-Boy! You told me the last time you visited me that you were going to do it and you did. That's the way to get the job done, son." OG wanted to hug D-Boy, but he knew the guards would object.

"Thanks Dad. But we came here to ask you some important questions about that day I got shot." D-Boy needed to know the answers.

"What you need to know?" OG got butterflies just thinking about that day.

"Who shot me? Was it a guy named Tone?" D-Boy stared into his Dad's eyes.

"Yes, it was Tone that shot you in the chest. The reason I said it was Jeff was because it would get me less time. I was facing twenty-five years to life. Tone escaped with his life that day because my gun jammed. I never brought it up to you because you were too young to understand back then. I figured I'd tell you one day. No time like the present," OG spoke quietly.

D-Boy was seething with anger. If he would've known this, he would've killed DJ T-1 earlier. The whole time he had a feeling about DJ T-1, but he had no idea it was because of this. He thought maybe he'd seen him in the streets or something.

"He tried to ruin my life. If it wasn't for D-Boy, I would still be in jail," Jason said.

"Hold on, I didn't get that part. How did D-Boy get you out?" OG asked.

D-Boy and Jason looked at each other. One of them had to tell OG the whole story. D-Boy preferred not to tell him, so Jason felt he had to. Even though he was still hurt by the whole incident, telling OG was his responsibility.

"Well, where should I start?" Jason closed his eyes to stop tears from pouring.

They both told the story from beginning to end, and how D-Boy got his hands on the footage that exonerated Jason.

"Good thing you got your hands on that video," OG said.

"Word! I was facing some time for that case. He even started a PayPal account in my DJ name. All the money went directly into that account. So it looked like I was working alone."

"He really had this all figured out. What're you going to do about this, D-Boy?" OG asked.

"I got something in mind, something real nice." D-Boys spoke through clenched teeth.

"I go to my parole board in two months. Hopefully, they'll let me go this time," OG said.

"Visiting time is over, people!" the CO announced.

"It was good to see you, Dad. I really hope you come home this summer. We have a lot of catching up to do," Jason said.

"No doubt. I miss you, Jason, and I want you to know that I'm very proud of you. You're the only man in the family that went the right route in life. For that I commend you, because I wasn't the best father. I should've kept the crime life far away from you guys but I didn't. That's how D-Boy got shot and ended up in the game." OG's eyes were misty, but he fought back the tears.

"It's not your fault, because Grandpa Joe and his father before him were all hustlers. You had no choice in the matter. The only thing we can do is change the game, now." Jason spoke from the heart.

"I guess I'll see you this summer when I make that parole board. I love you guys." OG hugged his sons and parted from the visiting room.

The drive back to NYC was eerily quiet. Both of them were plotting revenge on DJ T-1. D-Boy thought of ways to cleverly take DJ T-1 out without being caught. He knew he was being thoroughly watched by the FBI, one slip and he was gone for life. Whatever the cost, he was going to take DJ T-1's life for what he did to him.

"I know you're very angry about this DJ T-1 business, but don't let it mess with your head," Jason said right before getting out of the vehicle to enter his building.

"Don't worry, Jay. I got this one. You just get ready for the release of your album."

"Word. Bring Shoota down to the station tomorrow. He's going to be my first interview. I just got the green light to do interviews on my show now," Jason said.

"That's dope! So I'll see you tomorrow."

"Be safe, D-Boy." Jason spoke to him like they were kids again.

"You already know." D-Boy sped off from the curb.

AMERICAN D-BOY

Jason watched him drive down the block until his car was out of his view.

Be safe little brother, be safe.

* * * * *

D-Boy circled the block before he pulled into his garage. He entered the house from a door in the garage. It was similar to the garage in the house he lived in when he was shot. When he entered the house and turned the lights on, Agents Trenton and Kowalski were sitting on D-Boy's plush white leather couch.

"What the fuck are you doing in my motherfucking house?" D-Boy demanded. "This is some bullshit! Now the FBI is breaking and entering. I thought that was a crime."

"We're the FBI. We can do what the fuck we want. Now sit your black ass down," Agent Trenton commanded.

D-Boy knew he had to play it cool. They could murder him and get away with it. "What do you want? So you can get the fuck out of my house!"

"We know all about your little company, American D-Boy. And my buddy that arrested your big brother Jason is peeved that he beat the case on account of that video you came up with. Bravo! But if you think you're going to start your little record label, and that's it, you're off the hook. You have another thing coming! I'm going to put your black ass away even if it kills you!" Agent Trenton spoke with venom in his tone.

"That's what this is about? Me starting a legit company. I thought you'd be proud of me getting my life together. You know what your problem is, Agent

Trenton? You're a fucking HATER. You hate the fact that I'm young and black and I got more money than you. You hate your job because it doesn't pay shit. What you make in a year, I spend on dinners," D-Boy responded.

"That's the problem with you black guys. You think you can sell your drugs and make all that money and get out of the game like nothing ever happened. You have another thing coming! You had my Steph killed! By God, I'm going to make your life a living hell if it's the last thing I do." Agent Trenton spoke through clenched teeth.

"I'm sorry that Steph was killed. What do you want from me?"

"I want you to suffer the same way she did." Trenton stood up and walked to the door that he opened with his FBI issued skeleton key that was able to open any door. "See you real soon, D-Boy."

As soon as they left, D-Boy packed a suitcase and left his house. He had to lay real low. Agent Trenton made his point very clear. No matter what D-Boy did, Agent Trenton was going to put him in prison or try to murder him. D-Boy knew he was no match for the FBI. There was nowhere to run or hide from the Feds. Their jurisdiction was worldwide.

"I'm not going to let them win."

D-Boy drove his car as fast as he could on the Long Island Expressway headed to another one of his hideouts, where he kept all his money. This house was in eastern Long Island, in a town called Central Islip, on a secluded cul-de-sac. This shit was in the cut. D-Boy went there to get away from the game every now and then. No one knew about this house, except Jason. D-Boy had over $20 million in cash hidden in the house. It was his emergency money that he never touched. He had money stashed everywhere, but this was the most money he had stashed in one house.

"I'm not going out like a sucker! If I'm going down it's going to be in the blaze of glory in this bitch!" D-Boy stayed up all night planning and counting money.

CHAPTER 18
HOT 104 RADIO STATION

Te single from your up and coming album was the most requested song in NYC for ten weeks straight! How does that feel?" Jason asked Shoota, live on Hot 104 radio.

"It felt good. I mean, I'm a dude from the streets, so any recognition is dope for me!" Shoota responded.

"Who would you say is your biggest influence in the rap game today?"

"I don't really have an influence from the rap game. My influence is from the streets. My manager is who influences me. He's the reason I'm sitting here giving this interview. I look up to people that are real, that's why I made the John Gotti song, because John Gotti was real. He took what he wanted—he didn't wait for it to be passed to him. And he was from New York, so I wanted to bring that gangster shit back to the city. What better way than with John Gotti?"

"So what's next for Shoota?"

"I have that lead single 'More than a Playa' from your album, *The Awakening*, bubbling in the streets. Congrats to you on that. New York City, let me tell you, DJ Jay-Roc has one of the hottest albums for the summer coming out. You heard my single, the whole album is fire! *The Awakening* coming soon!" Shoota was always animated.

"Thank you, but we both have to thank the Don, D-Boy for making it all happen. Big shout out to American D-Boy Entertainment!" Jason was turned up now.

"No doubt! This is just the start of the end for you fake ass rappers!" D-Boy said with aggression. "This that Don, D-Boy in the flesh! New York City, stand up, Connecticut, New Jersey, Long Island, all over! American D-Boy is more than just music, it's a lifestyle!"

Jason was impressed with the way D-Boy turned up. He never saw him get amped like that. As soon as he finished speaking, the phone lines lit up with calls directed at D-Boy.

"You must be famous, D-Boy, because the phone lines just went crazy! And they're all asking for you. Do you have a moment to talk to the people?" Jason asked.

"Of course."

"Caller number one, you're on the line."

"What up, D-Boy? This is Jermaine from 109! I'm out here holding it down. I'm definitely feeling that American D-Boy movement! When is the album coming out?" Jermaine inherited doing most of the dirty work from D-Boy's empire, so he was doing quite well for himself.

"What up, boy? We was going to drop it on July 7th, but from the looks of it I may push the date up to May because the orders are crazy!"

"Let me know." Jermaine hung up.

"Caller number two, are you there?" I asked.

"Fuck American D-Boy! When I see you I'm going to murder you, pussy!" It was Andrew, the twin brother of Amos, the Haitian drug lord that Shoota assassinated.

"Word! You soft! I'm at the station. Come see me, pussy!" D-Boy responded.

"Say no more!" Andrew hung up.

* * * * *

"Load up the van, let's go see this loud mouth!" Andrew said to his men.

Andrew and three other Haitians stood up and stashed weapons on their person before leaving the apartment. They all headed for the same green minivan from the first attempt on D-Boy's life. They drove straight to the Hot 104 radio station and waited for D-Boy to come out.

"He think it's a game, but I'm not playing!" Andrew said as he cocked back his 9-millimeter and took the safety off.

* * * * *

D-Boy was inside the station with DJ Jay-Roc and Shoota. They just finished up the interview, and DJ Jay-Roc wrapped up the show. He was very concerned about the threats made on the radio. He knew D-Boy was used to threats, but this one sounded sincere.

"Do you think that caller is serious about meeting you at the station?" Jason asked D-Boy.

"I hope so, because I have something planned for them if they are," D-Boy responded with a smile.

AMERICAN D-BOY

D-Boy knew exactly who was on the phone, one half of the Haitian wonder twins, Andrew. Andrew knew that D-Boy put the hit out on Amos because of the failed attempt that killed Stephanie. They had an on-going feud that stemmed from D-Boy's beginning in the drug game. It all started when D-Boy's drug houses were making more than everybody else. So Amos had all of D-Boy's drug houses robbed. Then he tried to take them over, but that's when D-Boy paid thirteen gunmen to guard his houses and shoot anyone down with Haitian Amos and Andrew. The shootings went back and forth for years until one of the heads on the two-headed snake was cut off. This was a war.

Right after Andrew made his threats, D-Boy called Jermaine and told him to bring a small army to the station to handle this beef. Jermaine owed everything that he had become to D-Boy. In just two months, Jermaine went from making crumbs to eating the whole pie. To show his appreciation, Jermaine had ten shooters packed in two vans waiting outside right across the street from where the Haitians were parked.

"We're here, boss-man. When these niggas come out they're not going to know what hit them," Jermaine told D-Boy on the phone.

"I'm going to call you when I'm coming out of the building." D-Boy hung up.

D-Boy informed Shoota about what was about to go down. "I got ten armed men waiting for us to come out of the building. I know Andrew is out there. When they crawl out from under their rock to attack me, they're going to see why they shouldn't have ever got me started."

They headed for the exit. Right before he reached the door, D-Boy called Jermaine. "I'm stepping out of the building."

As soon as D-Boy and Shoota were on the street, Andrew and his three henchmen jumped out with masks on and guns out. They were walking toward D-Boy when shots rang out. Jermaine and his shooters saw the Haitians crossing the street with their weapons out. They immediately hopped out of their vehicles and let off shots directly at the Haitians. Two of Andrew's men hit the floor. Andrew was lucky to dodge bullets by using one of his men as a shield.

"Oh shit!" Andrew yelled out when the shots came out of nowhere.

D-Boy stood across the street in front of the building watching the whole scene unfold. D-Boy made sure he positioned himself right by the camera that was located by the entrance of the building watching him. When the police asked, D-Boy would have definitive proof that he had nothing to do with the shooting. He watched as Andrew and his men were rained upon with a barrage of bullets. They were like sitting ducks in the middle of the street.

It only took thirty seconds for Jermaine to take care of his business. "Let's go!" They got back into their vans and drove away from the scene.

Andrew got hit in his leg, but he'd live. Two of his men were dead, the other man was shot in his arm, but he'd also live.

"Fuck you, D-Boy! Fuck you!" Andrew looked up and saw D-Boy laughing at him from across the street.

AMERICAN D - BOY

"Come on, Shoota. Let's get out of here before the cops come." D-Boy and Shoota left the scene swiftly.

Andrew couldn't get away from the scene fast enough. When the cops got there, Andrew was on the floor next to his gun. There were a total of four guns lying next to four men. It was safe for the police to assume there was one gun per person, so Andrew was charged with felony gun possession. The minimum for Andrew was five years because he had prior felonies.

Even though D-Boy had fled the scene and he was on camera proving he wasn't a participant, he was still a suspect. The whole radio phone call was recorded, so it was no coincidence that there was a shooting right in front of the same station he'd just been threatened at. The police weren't stupid. Nevertheless, they couldn't charge D-Boy with anything.

The streets were going crazy about the war of words on the radio, and then the war of bullets that ensued. This type of episode is what made hood folklore. Not only did it make D-Boy a hood legend, but everybody in NYC and the tri-state area wanted to be down with American D-Boy Entertainment. They wanted the music, the clothing, anything that had to do with American D-Boy was just made super-hot.

Like any smart businessman, D-Boy saw an opportunity. There was a great demand for his product, so he needed to supply the people with what they wanted. D-Boy found a manufacturer to make American D-Boy hats, T-shirts, varsity jackets, and hoodies. He flooded NYC with his product, and in no time all the merchandise was sold. D-Boy purchased twice the amount on the second run, and the merchandise sold faster than the first batch.

The entire NYC, Long Island, Upstate, New Jersey, Connecticut and Philadelphia were rocking American D-Boy fashion. D-Boy drove through all the boroughs and saw how popular his brand had become overnight. He'd taken over his region, now it was time to put American D-Boy clothing in other states.

After selling so many units so fast, D-Boy was approached by a few distributors that wanted to partner with him. Out of the seven distribution companies that wanted to seal the deal, D-Boy chose a Brooklyn based company called CJ's Trucking Services. The reason he chose to do business with them was because the owner was a black man named Charlie Jackson that reminded him of his father, OG Jesse Jensen. Charlie was a tall, big dark skinned black man with a serious expression that said, 'I ain't no joke!' You could tell that Charlie was from the hood. D-Boy felt a street sense and a realness that he didn't pick up on when he spoke with the other bosses.

"Welcome to CJ's Trucking. We're going to do a lot of business. Where you from, Darius?" Charlie asked. D-Boy opted to use his government name, Darius, to do business with Charlie.

"I'm from South Side Jamaica Queens." D-Boy was always proud of his hood.

"That's where I'm originally from. I made it out by the skin of my ass. Reason I ask, is because I knew a fellow with your last name, his name was Joe, Joe Jensen. Do you happen to know a Joe Jensen?" Charlie asked.

AMERICAN D-BOY

"That's my grandfather!" D-Boy answered with excitement. "Wow, you know my grandfather!"

"How's old Joe doing these days?"

"He's good, still hustling. You can catch him betting on the horses down at Belmont Raceway."

"Yep, Joe and I used to highjack trucks, that's how I ended up in the trucking business. I said hell, why highjack the trucks when I can buy a few and ship out shit all day and make an honest living? I've been running this business for almost twenty-five years now, and I'm doing okay for myself." Charlie shook his head up and down as he strolled down memory lane.

"I knew it was a reason that I chose to do business with you. My spirit took to you. I'm from the streets, so I like to deal with real people." D-Boy spoke from the heart. "Do me a favor. All my true friends and associates call me D-Boy."

"D-Boy it is. We have a lot of work to do, D-Boy. You have so many stores that want your clothing that I got half of my trucks out delivering your product."

"Let's get to it."

Now that D-Boy had his American D-Boy clothing shipped across the country, it was selling like hotcakes in regions D-Boy wouldn't have expected it to sell. In four weeks, D-Boy made $800,000 and counting. The way it looked, this money was going to keep coming for a while. Now he had to drop this music that everyone was begging for: Jason's album, *The Awakening* was on the way!

There was one problem. George and his associates weren't happy with D-Boy handing the business over to Jermaine. George didn't like Jermaine, because he knew things about him that were classified. Jermaine was a confidential informant for the NYPD. A local rat, but small rats become big ones if allowed to live.

It wasn't Jermaine who was the major problem, it was Agent Trenton. He learned that Jermaine was running the show now, so he applied pressure to him. And just like he predicted, Jermaine burst like a water pipe—he started snitching on D-Boy for the FBI.

* * * * *

The waitress was cleaning up getting ready to close. "We'll be closing in twenty minutes gentlemen," she announced

"That rat bastard!" Sam said in a low voice.

"What did you say, Sam?" Jason asked.

"Oh, I said 'That rat bastard.' You know, for snitching on D-Boy."

"If I didn't know any better, it sounded like you took that shit personal," Jason stated.

"I guess I'm just so engrossed in the story that I took it personal," Sam said.

"This shit is intense, but if you thought it was crazy, this is where it gets ridiculous!" Jason paused. "Remember I told you that my brother's lawyer, John—that he used to have private investigators working for D-Boy?"

"Yeah, I remember that." Sam drummed his fingers against the table.

"Well, John found out about Jermaine snitching on D-Boy, and he found out some other deep shit."

"What?"

"He found out from doing some digging and searching that my brother's connect, George, was also an agent, but an agent of a different type. This motherfucker was the CIA the whole damn time!"

"Get the fuck out of here!" Sam said.

"And check this: he was getting the dope shipped in straight from Afghanistan from the government. My brother was selling heroin for the United States Government without knowing it."

"How did you find that out?"

"My brother told me. He was in fear of his life, and I was the only one he could confide in. That's how I know my brother's murder was more complex than meets the eye."

"It most definitely is," Sam agreed.

"That's why I told you this shit gets deeper."

ALAH ADAMS

CHAPTER 19

JOHN GILLESPIS'S OFFICE
Downtown, New York City

I need to talk to you in person. Meet me at my office in an hour," Attorney John Gillespie told D-Boy.

D-Boy got there in twenty minutes. "What's up, John? I got here as fast as I could."

"Listen, your boy Jermaine just signed up to work for Agent Trenton to put you away. They pressured him into committing suicide, knowing that every rat they employ to take you down winds up missing."

"Jermaine? That ungrateful bastard! He was a peon. I made him into the man he is and this is how he repays me? I should've left his bum ass on the corner where I found him!" D-Boy was very upset about Jermaine, but there was more.

"That's small shit compared to this." He handed D-Boy a file complete with pictures, secret missions, different disguises, places and events that this agent was working.

"This is George, my connect. What is this? Some type of joke." D-Boy was confused.

"Remember when I told you when we investigated George that he came out squeaky clean, but too squeaky clean. Most people have some glitch in their history, like a traffic ticket, or a late payment. Whenever someone is too clean it's because some agency is making sure it's that way."

"You sure know a lot about spy shit. Let me find out you're an agent yourself."

"You never know. But the dilemma is, they're going to kill you when they're done with you, like they do with all of their pawns," John said with confidence.

"Pawn! I'm not a fucking pawn! I'm a fucking Boss! I run shit!" D-Boy was offended.

"You *think* you run shit, but you were being played right from the start! You don't get it, do you? These people chose you to do the job. Sometimes it's because they know something about your past, or they just simply pick you to be IT, like a childish game of tag. You thought you were just selling all this heroin all this time because you were a Boss! Not by a long shot! They saw you and your brother a mile away on the corner and decided to use you in their little game. When they're finished with you, the news will say you were just another big time drug dealer that was taken down, or they'll find you dead somewhere. While the truth is, you were being used by the United States Government to move tons of their product in your impoverished neighborhood. If that's not a pawn, then I don't know what is."

That's when it really hit D-Boy like a sledge hammer. He knew John was right. He thought back to the day he met George, and how he just gave him and

Jason kilos with no questions, because he already knew. It all made sense to him. Many times Jason used to ask himself: Where the fuck is George getting all this pure dope from? It was like he was growing it, and that's because they were growing it.

"So what the hell am I supposed to do? I want out of the game, but you're telling me that it's impossible because they want me dead or in prison for the rest of my life. My twenty-fifth birthday is next month. I've always just wanted to live to twenty-five, that's all twenty-five years on the earth."

"I have a plan, but this plan has to be carried out with the utmost secrecy if it's going to work." John paused. "You're more like a son to me, and I watched you grow into the man you've become. That's why I'm going to help you."

* * * * *

"Sorry to interrupt, but we're closing now," the waitress announced to Jason and his guest.

"Okay, we were just finishing up," Sam replied.

"That was the last thing that D-Boy told me about that whole subject," Jason said after the waitress left.

"So you mean to tell me he didn't tell you what this grand plan was?" Sam asked.

"That's all he told me. Right after that, someone killed John. So I don't even think the plan was even put into effect."

"Hold on, the lawyer turned up dead?" Sam asked.

"He was gunned down in his Bentley by unknown assailants. We knew that it had to be the CIA or something, because the detectives said it was very professional. And it happened a week before my brother's murder, so it doesn't take a rocket scientist to figure out that D-Boy and John were killed by the same people."

"Excuse me, gentlemen, but you really have to go now," the owner said in a thick Jamaican accent.

"Well, I guess this is where we part ways," Jason said to Sam. "Here goes some money for your pocket. I know it's rough out here."

"I'm good. It was nice talking to you, Jason. Stay out of trouble and watch your back. The way that story ended, I wouldn't trust anyone." Sam shook Jason's hand and started walking fast.

"Wait!" Jason yelled, but Sam just kept walking. "That's strange. For a bum you sure do have some pride to turn down money. I was giving you twenty dollars."

That's when he knew that something wasn't right with Sam, so he followed him from a distance. Sam walked a block from the cemetery where he got into a black SUV with dark tinted windows. Jason was fortunate enough to see a cab parked with the driver in it.

"My man, I got a hundred dollars for you if you follow that black SUV before he pulls off," Jason said after getting in the backseat.

"You got it!" the cab driver responded.

The SUV drove fast. It was dipping and dodging through traffic as if he had sirens on. Then he jumped on the Long Island Expressway where he turned up his speed.

"You might have to give me another hundred for all this speeding," the cab driver said.

"I got you, just don't lose him!" Jason replied, while peeling another hundred dollar bill and handing it to him.

He checked his waist for his 9-millimeter. It was snug in the holster ready for some action if need be. Jason knew something was funny about Sam. He wasn't a bum, but the question was, who was he? With all the talk about CIA agents and shit like that, there's no telling who the fuck this dude was!

Whoever he was, Jason was about to find out.

CHAPTER 20

THE LONG ISLAND EXPRESSWAY

Sam took Jason on a wild goose chase on the Long Island Expressway. He got off on exit 55 in Central Islip. *Wait a minute! I know this town. This is where my brother had his big stash house. This is getting too weird right now. It isn't a coincidence that Sam is going to the same town that we just spoke about,* Jason thought.

"Do me a favor, most likely he's going to pull into a cul-de-sac. Don't pull in behind him. You can just let me out right before he turns into it."

"Okay, you got it, boss."

Just as Jason predicted, Sam turned into a cul-de-sac and parked in the driveway of the biggest house. It was the same house that D-Boy described to him. *What the fuck was Sam doing here? If his name is Sam at all, whoever the fuck he is. This shit is spooking me out, good thing I brought my gun with me.*

The cab driver let Jason out a block before the cul-de-sac. He crept up to the house and tried to look in the windows, but they were all tinted with curtains ensuring that no one could look through them. This

197

place was like a mini fortress the way the backyard was fenced in. Jason had his gun out just in case. He didn't want to get caught with his pants down. That's how you get fucked.

What his smart ass didn't know was that hidden cameras were all around the house and the whole block leading to a control room in the house. They were looking right at him. It was actually comical to them because it looked like Jason knew what he was doing, but of course he didn't.

* * * * *

"Do you see Jason creeping around the house? That's my fault for getting caught slipping. He followed me all the way here without me noticing," Sam said.

"I think we should just tell him the truth. You said he passed the test with flying colors."

"That's not part of the plan. We have to stick to it!"

"So what do we do, kill him? He knows where you're at, he's not stupid. He obviously knows that this is the stash house."

"Okay, but remember I was against it if anything goes wrong because of this."

They watched Jason on the screen trying to peep into the tinted windows of the house.

"Let him in. The neighbors are going to call the cops if they see him peeping through the windows like that. Then we will be bringing attention to ourselves, which is what we don't want."

"Okay, but remember I told you not to do this."

The front door opened. "Jason! Put the gun down and come in the house. There's something I have to tell you."

"Is that you, Sam! Or whatever your real name is! I'm not putting nothing down!" Jason yelled out.

"Just put the gun down and come in. No one is going to hurt you. There is something you have to know. Since you came this far, you might as well go all the way."

He came around to the front door and what he saw fucked up his whole psyche. "Hold up, you're not Sam, but you sound just like him. Wait, I know you! But that's impossible . . . they reported you dead!"

"Just come in so I can explain. We don't want the neighbors being nosey."

"John Gillespie! Wait, you were Sam?"

"Not so loud. Come in and I can explain everything."

That's when John grabbed Jason's arm and pulled him into the house and shut the door. The inside was like mission control with a bunch of computer screens lined up in a row. There were different countries on every screen, as if they were monitoring them. Jason stood looking around in amazement. Whatever this was, it was high tech.

"Now that you got me in this house, explain to me what the fuck is going on!" Jason demanded.

"Please have a seat. I think you need to be sitting for this," said John who was still dressed as Sam, minus the wig and the fake beard.

"I don't want to sit down. Just tell me what the fuck is going on!"

ALAH ADAMS

That's when a figure stepped out from the darkness. Jason stared at him as if he were a messiah at first, as if it couldn't be him. Then as he got closer and his eyes focused on his face. Jason knew exactly who he was.

"It can't be!"

Those were Jason's last words before he went blank and passed out.

CHAPTER 21

D-BOY'S SAFE HOUSE
Long Island, New York

Jason was out for two hours. He slept like a baby. When he woke up he thought everything was a dream. Jason thought the whole conversation with Sam and everything was just a dream, it couldn't be real. Then he saw him again.

"Wake up, sleeping beauty."

"It wasn't a nightmare. It really is you!"

"In the flesh, the one and only, Don D-Boy in the motherfucking building!" D-Boy announced.

"But how? I mean . . . how did you pull this off?" Jason asked.

"Okay where should I start?" D-Boy answered.

"The beginning would be good."

* * * * *

D-Boy got a call from George the day after John told him who he was. He was pissed off about D-Boy making Jermaine the head nigga in charge.

"I don't like this guy at all! He has a history of snitching for the NYPD! Did you know that?"

"I actually just found out that he was snitching on me. So yeah, I know," D-Boy answered sarcastically.

"You know? What else do you know?" George knew some things of his own. "I know your lawyer has been snooping around trying to find out who I am. And I know he knows something. Did he tell you yet?"

"It doesn't matter, you already have plans for me, don't you?"

"Listen, D-Boy, I've known you since you were fourteen years old. I grew to like you. Why don't you come down to the piers so we can talk about this?"

D-Boy knew right then and there that George was going to have him killed. "I'm good. We don't have anything to talk about."

"Don't do it like this, D-Boy. I'm warning you, things can get really ugly."

"It's already ugly."

"So I guess this is it," George said, sealing the deal that D-Boy was now a free agent.

"I guess so."

"Be safe out there, D-Boy. Be safe."

"You be safe too, Special Agent Greg Hummel. See, I know a lot about you too, Greg." That ruffled his feathers when D-Boy told him his real name. "You see, you're not the only one with pull in this world."

"So you want to play! So let's play!" He hung up the phone.

"The next day they shot up John's Bentley, but what they didn't know was that John always wore a bulletproof vest. Luckily for John, all the bullets hit the vest, so he lived. That's when John added himself to the plan and he had faked his death as well. They weren't going to stop until he was dead, so he might as well play dead."

"But how did you get the Queens County Coroner's office to issue an official certificate of death for both of you?" Jason asked, oblivious to anything.

"Money. We paid the coroner $1.5 million for two death certificates. That's more than he'll make in twenty years. He can retire from that and live a good life."

"But if your body wasn't in the car, then whose body was it?" Jason had to get to the bottom of this.

"It was Jermaine's body that blew up and was burned in the Benz."

"I don't get it. How?"

"I told Jermaine that I was getting out of the game and giving everything to him, but I needed him to do me one favor. Be at my house that morning to drive the Benz to the connect, and when the connect sees him in my Benz, he'd know that Jermaine was the new boss. He went for it and did exactly what he was told and that's how he ended up in the Benz that morning. Out of greed, he wanted to be the Kingpin. As they say, be careful what you wish for."

"But why did you have to go to such great lengths? Couldn't you have just exposed the CIA and the government, and exonerated yourself in the process?" Jason asked.

"They would've just swept it under the rug. They won't let the American Taxpayers know that this is a common practice of the CIA and our government. The people would rebel against the government, and the last thing they want is a full-fledged revolution. They're not going to let one fish spoil the whole sea.

So the only way out was for me to fake my own death. Now they are on to the next pawn."

"So now what are you going to do?" Jason asked.

"Before Stephanie was murdered she asked me to go away with her to Dubai or Sweden. I think I'll go to Dubai for seven years, and then come back under a different name and start over again."

"I can't believe you're still alive. You have everybody fucked up. Grandpa Joe was crying his old heart out. Dad was just trying to be hard, you know how he is. Shoota was distraught, you were his only friend."

"It don't stop! I want you and Shoota to hold down American D-Boy Entertainment in my absence. Just because I'm gone don't mean the label has to fold. I'll still be hands on from afar, just make the moves and we'll be good. American D-Boy clothing is at an all-time high with orders coming in from every state."

"No doubt. I can hold American D-Boy down! And I can send you money whenever you need it," Jason added.

"I'm not leaving just yet. I have some loose ends to tie up before I disappear."

Jason took a pregnant pause, and looked D-Boy in his eyes before speaking. "I never told you, but all these years I blamed myself for you getting shot at nine. Dad told me not to go in the garage that day, and I should've told you. Maybe you wouldn't have got shot."

"It's not your fault, everything happens for a reason. If I wouldn't have gotten shot I wouldn't become the man I am today." D-boy shook his hand

AMERICAN D - BOY

and hugged him at the same time, "Just do me one favor, keep all of this a super-secret. I know you can hold water that's why I needed you to know."

"Your secret is safe with me, D-Boy. I won't tell a soul."

"If it's anyone I trust, it's you, Jason. It isn't safe for you to be here. John, take Jason to his apartment."

"Sure," John replied.

"You really had me going with that bum disguise. I did say to myself, you seem familiar at one point. But you had me fooled."

"I just wanted to see how much you really knew," John responded.

"I guess this is goodbye, D-Boy," Jason said.

"Never goodbye, because you'll see me again. When you least expect it, I'll pop up on you. When you think of me, just smile, know that I'm alive and well somewhere living it up. All I want to do now is live, that's all. I just want to live and be free. Looking behind your back for enemies and the FBI and NYPD isn't living. I wasn't living my life. I was just surviving. This is the most freedom I've felt in my entire life. I'm actually happy that D-Boy is dead. It's time for me to be Darius for a change."

"You'll always be D-Boy to me, my little brother, D-Boy." Jason hugged D-Boy. "I love you, D-Boy. I'm so happy to know that you're alive and well." Jason spoke with eyes full of tears.

"I love you too, big bro. Now, you better catch that ride. I'll be around, just pay attention and you'll see me."

"See you later." Jason hopped in the black SUV with John and headed home.

"You really had me going with your disguise, John."

"I have everybody fooled, not just you." John looked at Jason. "This shit is very serious, Jason, and you have to take this secret to your grave. Your brother trusts you, so I trust you."

"Believe me, I think it's a blessing in disguise that D-Boy did this, because it wasn't going to end pretty for him. George and his people weren't going to let my brother live, neither was Agent Trenton or the Haitians."

"I got something for Greg AKA George. He tried to murder me. All the bullets hit me in the chest, breaking four ribs. Oh yeah, they're not the only ones that can put some shit together. Like D-Boy said, we have a couple of loose ends to tie up before we leave."

"I don't even want to know about it. I just want to live the rest of my life drama-free."

"I feel you. This is your stop. Hold your head up, and oh yeah, I almost forgot. Your brother left you a little parting gift to help with the label and just to make your life smoother. He knew you wouldn't take it from him, so he told me to give it to you once we got to your apartment."

"That damn D-Boy! He really does know me." Jason paused and shook his head. "How much did he give me?"

"I think it's only $1.5 million."

"One point five million dollars in cash! That's like three large duffle bags!" he complained.

"That's exactly three large duffle bags that are in the back. You're a big, strong young man. I'm sure you can manage it."

"I want to thank you for looking out for my little brother," Jason said.

"Don't mention it. D-Boy is like a son to me. Besides, I was about to retire anyway," John responded. "Remember, this stays between us."

"You already know." Jason gave John the serious nod. "See you later, and tell D-Boy I love him."

"Sure thing."

John unlocked the trunk, and Jason lifted the heavy bags of money up four flights of stairs to his humble one bedroom apartment.

When Jason opened the door to his apartment, the lights were off but there were candles lit. R. Kelly's classic "Bump & Grind" was playing low in the background. A beautiful black Queen lay on the couch. She must've fallen asleep waiting for him. Jason almost forgot he gave her the keys to his apartment. He put the bags of money in his walk-in closet, then he sat on the couch and rubbed her hair.

"Wake up, baby. I'm home," Jason said sweetly in her ear.

"Damn, baby, what took you so long? I wanted to surprise you, that's why I didn't call you. I must've dozed off," Tracy replied.

"It's a long story, one I don't care to go into right now. Let me take a shower, and we can share the rest of the night together."

Yeah, Jason bagged Tracy Spencer from Hot 104. What could he say? He's a sucker for love. Besides,

Tracy and Jason were made for each other. Come to find out, Tracy used to DJ when she went to NYU. They had so much in common that it scared him sometimes. They finished each other's sentence and everything! Tracy was truly Jason's soul mate.

"Damn, that was a long shower!" Tracy said playfully.

"I know. I had to wash off all the bullshit from today."

"I know it must've been hard burying your little brother," Tracy said with concern.

"It was the hardest thing I ever had to do, but I stayed strong for D-Boy."

"Well, I need something strong, and long." Tracy kissed him gently on his cheek.

"What might that be?"

"I don't know, let me see." She reached for his penis, and from there it was on.

They made love all night long! For the first time Jason made real love with a woman. They made sweet, old fashioned LOVE!

The next day Jason woke up and took a shower and got dressed in his American D-Boy shirt and hat and looked at himself in the mirror. For once he appreciated his life and what he'd become. He knew he had a long way to go, but his path was clear. He missed D-Boy, but knowing that he was really alive made him smile. He'd learned a lot in the past year, now he was ready to live to the fullest. Just like D-Boy.

American D-Boy!

EPILOGUE

One Year Later . . .
Hot 104 Radio Station

If you're just tuning in, it's the magnificent DJ Red Zone, and we have the one and only DJ Jay-Roc, aka The Gold DJ, CEO of American D-Boy Entertainment here live at Hot 104!"

"What's going on NYC, Long Island, New Jersey, Connecticut and the whole world? It's your boy DJ Jay-Roc, rocking non-stop!"

"Let's get right into it. How does it feel to go from a DJ here at Hot 104, to being the boss of your own label and having five gold singles from your debut album, *The Awakening*?" DJ Red Zone asked.

"It feels great! I mean, I worked hard to get everything I got. Just a year ago I was sitting right in that same chair doing the same show. But the transition from DJ to mogul was all because of my little brother D-Boy, God bless the dead. He left me the blueprint and I built an empire!"

"Not only are you doing numbers, but Shoota, Top Notch, and Rick Rude are also topping the charts! What's the formula for their success?"

"We came in the game with a solid brand with the American D-Boy clothing line, so it wasn't hard to push out good music with that stamp on it. The people understand our movement, so they support anything we do. We run the streets with this rap shit, hands down! That's the real formula." Jason was on his boss shit today.

"So what's next for DJ Jay-Roc?"

"I'm about to drop my new album, *Positive Energy* in the fourth quarter, like November. Then I got the young brother, Top Notch's album, *Evolution* dropping right before my album in the fall, back to school season! And I just signed this talented artist name Bao' Mao'. He's coming with that fire! And we're about to shoot a movie with everyone that's signed to American D-Boy as the stars."

"That's going to be big! Let me know when you do auditions. I can act!" DJ Red Zone was reaching.

"No doubt, I'll definitely let you know."

"Oh yeah, congratulations! You're a new father." DJ Red Zone was overexcited.

"Yeah, shout out to my baby boy, Darius. We call him Little D-Boy. And my beautiful wife, Tracy."

"Okay, you named your first child after your brother. That's what's up! I know D-Boy would be very proud of you for continuing to build the label after his demise."

"Most definitely. Today makes a year that D-Boy was taken away from us." Jason had to take a pause. He knew his brother was alive, but he still missed him.

"Damn! It feels like it was yesterday when the news of his murder spread throughout the city. It was like the president died or something, the way people reacted to D-Boy's death in New York. How do you deal with his passing?"

Jason had to think about this question. Although he knew Darius was alive, D-Boy was dead. That's what Jason had to tell himself to keep up the façade for this whole year. A lot had happened in a year. He wished D-Boy were here to celebrate the success of his brainchild, American D-Boy.

"I believe when a person passes, their spirit is still with us. Just because we can't see them in the physical, doesn't mean they don't still exist on the spiritual plane. So I know D-Boy is still with us in spirit, somewhere listening and watching me like my guardian angel. I want you to know you'll never be forgotten!

"Long Live D-Boy!"

- THE END??? -

ALAH ADAMS

American D-Boy
Reading Group Discussion Questions

1.   How did you like the experience of the twist in the plot? Describe how it made you feel?

2.   Did the many twist in the plot catch you off guard or did you see them coming?

3.   Do the main characters come to life? Did you understand each characters traits?

4.   If so which characters did you like the most? Explain what you liked most about him or her.

5.   Did you like the transition from dope dealer, to DJ at the radio station theme?

6.   Did you feel that Hip Hop was a strong theme in the plot? If so, how did that make you feel?

7.   Was American D-Boy a faced paced plot driven book? Or did it drag on before it picked up?

8.   At the end when D-Boy was explaining how he was able to fake his death, did it seem realistic? Or too far-fetched?

9.   What did you think about the theme where the CIA was supplying D-Boy with heroin? How did it make you feel?

10.   Did American D-Boy enlighten you in any way? Did it broaden your perspective about life?

ALAH ADAMS

About the Author

Alah Adams isn't just a published Author, he's a songwriter/rapper, and an actor/screenplay writer. Right before press he just added clothing designer to his list of talents by launching a clothing line called American D-Boy, named after this novel.

After serving 7 years in a New York State prison for selling drugs, Alah started Gully Multimedia, LLC and self-published his first novel Banana Pudding. Alah is currently working on a Hip Hop television series with the infamous rap video film company Street Heat TV called Battle Kings.

Alah Adams resides in Long Island, New York.

T.H.O.T!

THAT HO OUT THERE

BY
ALAH ADAMS

Prologue

Vinny hid in the closet of the plush condo he purchased for Chasity. He shed tears as he listened to the sounds of Torian pounding her vagina as if he were killing her.

"Oh my god!" Chasity screamed out in ecstasy. "You are the best! Keep fucking me!"

I can't believe this is happening. I trusted her with everything and this is how she repays me, Vinny thought as he cocked back the 45 caliber ACP pistol. *I knew I should've listened to Rocco.* Vinny sniffled.

"What is that noise?" Torian asked, stopping midstroke after hearing a clicking of some kind. "It sounds like somebody is in the closet."

Torian dismounted Chasity and grabbed his pants where he'd concealed his 9-millimeter. Before he could grip his weapon, Vinny rushed out of the closet busting shots.

Bang! Bang! Bang!

The first shot hit Torian in his shoulder, pushing him two steps back. He fell to the floor about two feet from his 9-millimeter. He lay there not making a sound, pretending to be unconscious, yet inching his hand toward his gun. The other two bullets landed in the headboard right by Chasity's head.

"Vinny!" she yelled. "Baby, please, put the gun down. It's not what it looks like."

"That's all you have to say!"

Bang!

He let off a shot right by her head. Tears streamed down Vinny's face. "I gave you everything! I took you from living in motels selling your ass, to a condo and a BMW! And this is how you repay me!" He lunged toward her as if to strike her with the butt of his gun.

"Wait! I can explain!" She smiled in an attempt to calm him down.

"I don't want to hear it!" Vinny pointed the gun at Chasity. "I should kill you!"

Torian got his hand on his gun, but he didn't have a clear shot at Vinny because of the angle. Vinny moved closer to Chasity, putting the gun to her head, which gave Torian the perfect advantage. Just as Torian's index finger pressed on the trigger, Vinny saw him in his peripheral, turned and let off two shots in rapid succession.

Bang! Bang!

One of the shots hit Torian in his chest, but not before Torian let off three shots at the same time. Two shots hit Vinny in his neck, causing him to slump to the ground while gurgling on his blood. Both men lay on the floor, gravely injured.

Chasity stood viewing the carnage. She couldn't believe what had just happened. It was so surreal that she closed her eyes.

"This isn't real," she told herself. "Snap out of it!"

When she opened her eyes, both men were dead. At that moment, her mind had been stripped of its ability to reason. Disoriented, she gazed at both bodies as if they were illusions. Chasity didn't speak or blink and remained motionless. The sounds of Suffolk County police officers entering the room with their guns drawn, brought her out of her trance.

"Get on the floor with your hands behind your head!" the officer yelled.

Unresponsive and stark naked, Chasity just stood there.

The officer, seeing her blank expression, realized that she posed no immediate threat. He slowly moved toward her, took one of the blankets that lay on the bed, and covered Chasity's body. The other officers looked at the two bodies on the floor. They glimpsed the 45 caliber ACP next to Vinny, and the 9-millimeter lying next to Torian.

The first officer put his gun away and grabbed Chasity by her shoulders. "Miss, are you all right?"

She remained upright but in a catatonic-like state, experiencing the effects of extreme shock.

After a half hour, the officer took her to a police vehicle while the homicide squad combed over the scene. It was cut and dry, two men shot each other to death over a woman. It didn't take long for them to surmise the situation.

Chasity was escorted to the precinct where she was placed in a small interrogation room. She was still in shock, but no longer catatonic. The officer gave her some clothes to put on before they left. Now she sat in the cold, gray room confused as to what was really going on. The door suddenly opened, and in walked a female with a detective badge hanging from her neck.

"How are you doing? My name is Detective Jennifer Colon." She wore a serious expression as she glanced at the paperwork she held. "Miss Chasity Johnson, that's you, right?"

She took a few seconds before speaking, "Yes, that's me."

"Okay, Chasity. Can you tell me what happened today?" She slammed the door. Detective Colon's demeanor was icy toward Chasity. She appeared to be upset about something, and stood looking down at Chasity with disgust. Her long, dark hair fell over her face, hiding her expression. She moved her hair aside and stared at Chasity with unfriendly eyes before taking a seat.

Chasity's eyes widened, but they didn't blink. She remained quiet and seemed to be regressing into her guilty conscience.

"Take your time, take a deep breath," Detective Colon suggested. "If you want me to help you, I need you to tell me how this happened . . . from the beginning."

Slowly, Chasity took in a deep breath and let it out just as measured.

"It all started a year ago when I first met Vinny . . ."

Detective Colon pressed record on the mini video recorder that sat on a tripod. "Okay, take your time. Start from the beginning."

Chasity closed her eyes, but when she opened them she began speaking. "I'm not at all what I appear to be. I have deceived many men by using my looks and my body to lure them into my world of lust. The warning signs were all around me, telling me to stop, telling me that there was danger ahead. But I didn't listen, and now two men are dead. And it's all because of me."

Chasity paused and gazed into the camera wearing a slight smile.

CHAPTER 1
A Sucker, With a Capital 'S'!

Bay Shore Motor Inn
Bay Shore Long Island, New York

CHASITY

"I don't give a fuck about you or anything that you do!" Chasity sang along with Big Sean to his new single, "I Don't Give a Fuck!" as it blasted on the radio. "This is my new anthem! Because I really don't give a fuck about these niggas!" Chasity spoke with passion while she inhaled a huge blunt, then she passed it to Kat.

"My sentiments exactly!" Kat replied as she reached for the blunt and inhaled.

Chasity sat on the bed scantily clad in red Victoria's Secret matching bra and panties. She had her laptop open checking her traps on the infamous "Front Page" website. Front Page was a way for tricks and 'hos to link up via the Internet. She liked to use the word *Trap* to describe the way she enticed weak men into her web of deceit and pleasure. Chasity was a modern day call girl, a prostitute, otherwise known in the hood as a T.H.O.T, an acronym for 'That Ho Out There.'

"The day just started, and I already have three new traps lined up. At $250 a piece that's $750 for about an hour's worth of work," Chasity said to Kat, her best friend and partner in crime.

"The way these tricks be coming so fast, you can cut that hour into thirty minutes worth of work." Kat inhaled the blunt and then passed it to Chasity.

"I got this one trick that fucks me for the whole hour! I think that nigga be on something before he comes here," Chasity responded.

The days of 'hos walking the strip trying to catch a date were a thing of the past. Nowadays these young thots knew how to use the Internet to their advantage by posting provocative pictures with an implied message. The tricks were up on the new technology, so they went on the sites looking for new 'hos to trick on. That cut out the pimp and the risk of being seen by detectives walking on the 'Thot Trot,' the blocks where primitive thots walk trying to catch a trap.

Chasity and Kat were two of the best 'thots' in Long Island. Both women were voluptuous with gorgeous faces. They were divas, so they always adorned their heads with expensive wigs, kept their toes and nails done, and wore the newest designer labels. They were known to frequent the VIP section in the hottest clubs, buying their own bottles, balling out!

Tall with big brown eyes, Chasity inherited a honey-brown complexion from her Puerto Rican mother and Black father. Her pearly white teeth were esthetically pleasing to the eye. When she got dressed up, people often told her she resembled Beyoncé. She kept her stomach flat which made her firm, size 38D cups stand at attention. Chasity was a complete 10!

Kat was a bit shorter, but her ass wasn't. Ass for days, flat stomach, and a nice amount of tits, she was a little darker than Chasity, but people always mistook them for sisters. Chasity and Kat didn't see the resemblance, but they chalked it up to them being around each other so much that they started looking alike. As a team, they were like the dynamic duo.

Kat's phone went off. "That's my number one trap texting me. He's here. I'm going to my room to take care of him."

"Okay, my trap should be here shortly. I'll see you for lunch," Chasity said.

"That sounds like a plan."

Kat went two rooms down. They always got rooms close to each other for safety. Being that they didn't have pimps to protect them, they both kept revolvers close to them at all times. In the past they had been violated by tricks who knew they didn't have pimps.

Shortly after Kat left the room, Chasity's new trap knocked on the door. She knew it was him, so she sprayed herself with Chanel No. 5 before answering. Her motto was 'Go above and beyond to please' to ensure that her traps stayed loyal.

She answered the door in her Victoria's Secret undergarments.

"Hi. Vinny, right?" she asked, showing her perfect rows of white teeth.

"Yes, I'm Vinny. You're Cherry?" he asked in a nervous tone. *Wow! This chick is fucking beautiful! I hit the jackpot!* he thought.

Chasity saw that Vinny was stuck in thought standing in the doorway. She glanced at him from head to toe quickly before inviting him in. "You can come in and make yourself comfortable."

Short, fat, and Italian with slicked black hair, Vinny wasn't quite the looker, but he was very charming. He possessed a gentleman-like quality that made him attractive to women. He was like a knight in shining armor, without the shining armor.

Chasity had a sixth sense for men that were enamored by her. Her 'sucker for love' meter dinged off the charts with this new guy. At first sight she could tell he was smitten by her beauty. She was a pro at tempting men, so she knew exactly how to handle him.

"So, Vinny, what do you do for a living?"

"I'm in the construction business."

"Oh, I see, construction. Are you a foreman?" she asked.

"No. I own a construction business with my family." Vinny was visibly nervous. He kept rubbing his hands together in an attempt to calm his nerves.

Get it together Vin! He thought.

"It must be nice to work with your family."

"Not all the time, but it beats working for some Joe Schmo."

Chasity stared in his eyes and he got weak. She moved closer and he almost jumped. Normally she would ask for money up front, but she was playing him all the way to the bank. She smelled money like a shark smells blood.

She noticed his nervousness. "Relax, I'm not going to bite you. Unless you tell me to." She smiled and Vinny seemed to unwind a bit.

Getting right down to business, Chasity unbuckled his belt and pants and pulled his penis out. Vinny almost freaked out, breathing heavily. Immediately, she took him into her mouth as if her life depended on it. The force with which she sucked his penis made Vinnie's toes curl in seconds. She felt his sperm swelling up in his balls early, so she slurped with more ferociousness.

"Oh my God!" Vinny yelled out in ecstasy. "I'm coming!"

"Mmmmm! It tastes so good!" Chasity said as she lapped up his semen.

Vinny's eyes were rolling around in his head. "You're the best! I mean that."

"Never had any complaints."

"No, really. No woman has ever made me come that fast from sucking my dick before." Vinny took out five 100 dollar bills. "I know you said it was only $250, but you were so good I'm giving you double!"

I got him! Hook, line, and sucker! she thought. "Aww, you don't have to do that. You're so sweet, Vinny."

"No, I want you to take it. I want to see you every day if that's possible?" He was panting and sweating. He looked at her like a puppy that needed attention from its master.

"Of course you can, silly!" Chasity laughed. "You're so funny!"

"Can we just cuddle for a minute?" Vinny knew that was a weird question.

"Sure, baby. Take your clothes off and get under the covers. You still have about fifty minutes left."

Vinny did as he was told. He curled up and went to sleep with Chasity as if she were his wife. He was officially open.

Damn this nigga hooked already, and I didn't even throw this tight, wet pussy on him yet. Chasity thought. She let him sleep for an hour, then she woke him up.

"Wake up, sleepy head. Time to go."

"Damn, I was out of it." Vinny got up and put his clothes on. "So, I'll see you tomorrow at the same time?"

"If that's what you want, honey. I'll be here waiting for you, baby." She kissed him on the cheek.

Vinny finally left, and she watched him walk away to see what model car he drove. When he sat comfortably in a new jet black BMW 650i convertible, she knew she'd hit the jackpot. *Everything about Vinny screams money. And I want it all!*

Just as Vinny was leaving, Chasity got a text from her next client: *I'm pulling in right now.*

Okay, I'm ready.

She went to the bathroom and rinsed her mouth out with mouthwash and brushed her teeth. As she was finishing up, there was a knock on the door.

She answered it with the same smile as before. "Hi, John. Come in and make yourself comfortable."

John was a regular, and he wasn't a two-minute man. He was smart enough to pop a Viagra before his weekly appointments. Also, John wasn't rich. He was just a truck driver with an appetite for young thots. Every week he would spend his hard earned money on one hour of pleasure.

Tall and dark-skinned, the older Black man had been married twice and divorced twice. Although he came equipped with a ten-inch penis, his last girlfriend cheated on him with his best friend, and that's when he decided to just deal with women like Chasity and call it a day. For him it was less headaches and no commitment, that's what he enjoyed most about the situation.

John didn't waste any time. Chasity knew that John came to put in work, so she prepared her mind for the task of getting fucked hard. He took his clothes off and put his stiff penis in her mouth and shoved it down her throat. She moaned in protest, but she didn't stop him from manhandling her. There was something about his roughness that Chasity enjoyed. He didn't treat her like the doll she appeared to be. John treated her like the thot he knew she was. And Chasity loved it.

For fifty-five minutes straight, John pummeled her vagina before ejaculating and leaving her sore. "I'll see you next week, same time." John was a man of few words. He was dressed and out the door minutes after he was done.

Chasity had twenty minutes before her next appointment and she wasn't ready. She dragged her sore body to the bathroom and took a long, hot shower. As she rubbed her vagina, she thought about her first trick Vinny. *I knew Vinny was a breadwinner! What if*

AMERICAN D - BOY

I can entice Vinny to the point where he'll just take care of me, and I don't have to be fucking like this for money? It would be nice to be taken care of for a change. She became so engrossed in her thoughts that she lost track of time.

There was a knock on the door. Her next trap was on time.

"Hold on, I'm coming!" she shouted from the shower as she got out and dried off. *Got to get this money. It's all in a day's work.* Chasity opened the door.

"Hi Paul. Come in and make yourself comfortable."

Detective Colon paused the video. "So, you met Vinny on the Front Page website. I'm going to do you a favor."

"What's that?"

"I'm not going to arrest you for prostitution. Let's just pretend like I don't know anything about that. I'll erase the whole first part when we're done, so we both won't get into hot water."

Detective Colon pushed record on the video. "Continue." *Murderous slut! You just couldn't keep your fucking cunt-hole closed!*

CHAPTER 2

No Honor Among Thots!

Construction Site
Dix Hills, Long Island

"Yo, I'm telling you, man. This chick was gorgeous with a body like a goddess!" Vinny said to his cousin Rocco.

"Oh yeah. You said you found her on that website," Rocco responded.

"Yeah, Front Page. She goes by the name Cherry. Her pics do her no justice. She looked okay, but in person she was dynamite!" Vinny smiled just thinking of her. "I'm not sharing this one with you this time. She's all mine," he said in a serious tone. In the past they shared prostitutes.

"Well, let me know if she has a friend or something. I'll fuck around a little. By the way, how's Jenny and the kids?" Rocco asked.

"She's okay. The kids are driving me nuts with their bullshit. I bust my ass so that they'll have everything, and they still get into trouble. I'm going to court right now because Anthony stole clothes from the mall. Funny thing was, he had a pocket full of money when they caught him." Vinny shook his head just thinking about his troubles at home.

"We did worse when we were his age. Sounds like he needs attention or something."

"Then you wonder why I need Cherry's services. In fact, I'm going to see her when this job is done."

"You've been seeing her every day. She must have some good pussy. You can't get enough."

"I just met her last week. I can't explain how she makes me feel. It's like she's dedicated to pleasing me to the utmost, Rocco. I could marry this broad, I'm telling you. Ho or no ho, I love this chick."

"Now you're talking crazy, Vinny! You have a wife and kids. You can't throw that away for some two-bit slut you met online at some prostitution website!" Rocco fumed.

"It's my life and I can do what I want," Vinny spoke calmly, but he got into Rocco's face. "If you have a problem with it, you don't have to fuck with me!"

"Oh yeah! So you're going to choose some cunt over your own flesh and blood?" Rocco pushed Vinny in his chest with both hands causing him to stumble two steps back.

"If that's how you want to put it!" Vinny replied, catching his balance.

"Fuck you, Vinny! One day you're going to eat those words!" Rocco stormed off and got into his Ram truck and sped off from the construction site, leaving a small dust storm in his wake.

"Fuck me! No, fuck you!" Vinny took out his phone and dialed Chasity.

****

"Suck that dick! Oooo! That shit feels soo good!" Sincere said while Chasity gave him fellatio.

As she was performing, her cell phone went off. She saw that it was Vinny. Without taking her mouth off Sincere's penis, Chasity answered the phone with one hand while holding his dick with the other.

"Hello, Cherry?" Vinny said like an excited teen.

She removed his penis from her mouth. "Hey baby," she said those two words then put his dick back where it had been.

"I need to see you."

"Mm-kay."

"Can I come by like right now?" Vinny asked in a desperate tone.

"Sure . . ." *Suck, suck.* ". . . I'm here, baby." *Suck, suck.*

Sincere had to muster the strength not to make a noise because he wanted to moan in ecstasy. He knew he had to keep his composure, so he closed his eyes and covered his mouth with one hand.

"I'll be there in twenty minutes."

"Okay, baby . . ." *Suck, suck, suck.* "I'm going to get freshened up for you." She hung up.

"Yeah! I like that freaky shit! Talking on the phone while sucking on that cock! Ooo, you so nasty!" Sincere was close to ejaculating.

"We have to cut this shit short today, Sincere."

"What you mean? I gave you a whole ounce of loud for my usual hour. If you cutting my time in half, I'm giving you half an ounce!"

"Shut up and nut in my mouth!" She took him to the back of her throat, nearly swallowing him. "There it goes!"

Sincere filled Chasity's mouth up with warm cream. "Ooo! And you swallow! You so nasty!"

"Now get your ass out of my room!" she demanded.

"I was just playing. You can keep the whole ounce. You always take care of the god. For real!" Sincere pulled up his pants and then buckled his belt. "I'll see you next week, and we can square off with that extra half an hour."

"Whatever, Sincere!" She slammed the door in his face.

Chasity rolled up a gigantic blunt of Sincere's top shelf marijuana and lit it up. She had a bottle of Henny lying on the dresser. Chasity grabbed it and guzzled. She took three more pulls of the blunt, then another swig before the room started spinning. Satisfied with the desired effect, she smiled and grabbed her laptop.

"Damn, a bitch got four new traps! This shit don't stop! My shit stay lit!"

She turned on the radio and Bobby Shmurda's "Hot Nigga" played on the airwaves. Chasity turned the volume up to maximum capacity.

"Hey! Hey!" she shouted, doing the signature '*shmoney dance*' that went with the song. "I send a little thot /to get the drop on 'em!" She sang along with Bobby to her favorite part of the song.

A few minutes later, she put the blunt out and quickly took a shower before Vinny got there. Like clockwork, Vinny was at the door knocking with flowers in his hand. Chasity opened the door.

"Hey baby!" Chasity paused. "You brought me flowers! You're so sweet, Vinny."

Vinny handed her a dozen long stemmed red roses while blushing, "It's the least I can do for the most beautiful girl in the world."

"You're going to make me cry." Chasity was fronting. She really wanted to laugh.

This nigga is a sucker with a capital S!

"I was thinking, instead of us having sex, I'd like to take you to a fancy Italian restaurant for dinner,"

Vinny said nervously. He wasn't sure how she'd respond.

"I am kind of hungry. Sure, let's go to dinner."

"Great!" Vinny was suddenly excited. "I'll wait for you in the car."

Chasity got dressed and waltzed out to Vinny's car. "Nice car, Vin!"

"You like it?"

"I love it! This is the new BMW 650i convertible. Who wouldn't love it?"

"It's yours." Vinny looked at her with a serious expression.

"You're joking, right?" Chasity didn't find it funny.

"I'm as serious as cancer. I have six cars. It's nothing for me to give you this one if it makes you happy."

Chasity hugged him tight. "Oh, Vinny! I can't believe it!"

"Believe it, doll face! If it makes you happy, then it's yours."

"I don't know what to say." Chasity was at a loss for words.

"You can start with 'Thank you, Vinny.'" Vinny smiled then started the car and began driving toward their destination.

When they arrived at Mama Leona's, Chasity was smiling from ear to ear. She looked at her new BMW once she made her exit. Slowly, she walked around it, examining every curve. She still couldn't believe Vinny just gave her a BMW.

I'm going to stunt hard in this fucking car! Haters beware!

Vinny watched her admiring the vehicle. "Anything to make you happy, doll face."

They strolled into the restaurant and were seated in a cozy booth. The waitress came and they placed their orders. Of course, Chasity had to have alcoholic drinks with her meal. Vinny didn't mind, he was in heaven just being in Chasity's presence.

The food came and Chasity dug in like an inmate just set free.

"You really were hungry," Vinny said, noticing her eating frenzy.

"No, it's not that. I was smoking some good weed right before you came, so I'm hungry because of that."

"I was thinking, maybe you should move into one of my condos. It's a gated community, so no one gets in without your permission. You'll be safer that way. I worry about you staying in those cheap hotels every night."

"Aww, you're the best, Vin!" She grabbed his hand and squeezed it. "No man has ever cared about me this much." She faked tears.

"Don't cry, baby." Vinny was sincerely touched. "It's the least I can do for the woman that makes me feel like a million bucks every day."

"I really don't know what to say."

"Say you'll move your stuff in tomorrow."

"Okay, I'll move my stuff in tomorrow." She smiled and that sealed the deal.

An hour and a half later, the two finished eating. On the way to the car, Vinny passed her the keys to the BMW. "You drive."

Chasity jumped in the driver's seat and started up the expensive vehicle. The engine growled when she pressed the gas pedal. She got moist just feeling the car's power.

"Where do you want me to go?" she asked.

"You can take me home and I'll see you tomorrow." Vinny gazed at her with infatuation in his eyes.

Chasity adjusted the seats to accommodate her long legs, "You're dead serious about giving me this car, aren't you?"

"I surely am."

"What do you want in return for the car?" Chasity knew the car came with a price.

"I just want you to be mine when you're with me. I know what you do and I respect it. All I ask is when you're with me to treat me like the only man in the world, and I'll be cool with that."

"So let me get this straight. As long as I treat you like my man, you're okay with what I do for a living?" She was confused, because no man would wife a thot.

"Exactly!" Vinny said with enthusiasm.

"Okay, you got a deal." Chasity hugged him and kissed him passionately on his lips.

The kiss shocked him. "Wow! That was a great kiss. May I have another?"

"You sure can." This time she stuck her tongue all around his mouth.

"I can get used to this."

Vinny showed her where to drop him off, and she drove back to her room. When she pulled up, Kat was standing in the doorway to her room watching Chasity get out of the BMW.

"Whose car is that?" Kat asked as Chasity approached her.

"It's mine." Chasity tilted her head smugly. "Just got it from Vinny."

"Are you serious?" Kat couldn't believe it.

"He just gave it to me after he took me to dinner at Mama Leona's."

"I love Mama Leona's! I'm hating right now!"

"Bitch! Don't hate, congratulate!" Chasity got out and locked the car. "I got some bomb ass loud from Sincere today. You want to smoke?"

"Hell yeah! I didn't smoke nothing all day."

AMERICAN D - BOY

They walked in the room and started smoking and drinking the rest of the Henny.

"Guess what?" Chasity asked.

"Let me see, homeboy is buying you a house?"

"Close. He's moving me into a condo tomorrow."

"Damn! This guy is serious. See if he has a friend or something. I'm trying to come up too," Kat said.

"I most definitely will ask him if he has a guy friend for you."

"Let me know."

They smoked and drank until they both passed out on Chasity's bed. When Chasity was completely out, Kat got up and looked at her phone. She saw the number for Vinny, and she memorized it and put it into her phone. *You're not the only one that can throw it down on a trap,* Kat thought as she went to her room. She thought about calling Vinny, but decided against it. *I'll just call him tomorrow after Chasity leaves.*

She almost felt guilty about snaking Chasity, but that feeling passed quickly. *Just like there's no honor among thieves, there's no honor among thots either.*

CHAPTER 3
Promoted!

Fairfield Condos

Vinny kept his promise and moved Chasity into his condo. She came with nothing but a suitcase full of clothes. The whole condo was already beautifully furnished with an eggshell white leather couch in the living room and glass end tables. A 70-inch flat screen TV hung from the wall. The bedroom was even more captivating. The balcony overlooked a manmade lake that nestled in the middle of the complex. To put it short, Chasity had just got promoted in life.

"This is beautiful, Vinny!" She hugged him tight. "How could I ever repay you?"

"Well, you can start by giving me a blowjob."

"I thought you'd never ask."

Chasity did what she does best. When she was done, Vinny went to sleep, leaving her to think about her new condo. Never in her life had she dwelled in anything this lavish before. Chasity came from a poor family with no father. She had two sisters and no brothers, and she didn't get along with her sisters.

Chasity fucked both of her sisters' men, which led to her being excommunicated by them.

Her mother, Catherine was an alcoholic and didn't care about her daughters. They were left to fend for themselves. That's how Chasity ended up in the streets selling her body. She was introduced to prostitution at the early age of sixteen by an older girl named Nancy. Nancy taught Chasity everything she knew about the sex trade. When Nancy got arrested for boosting, Chasity stepped her game up and became the thot that she was.

As Chasity reflected on her past, shivers shot up her spine. One incident always haunted her. When Chasity was nine years old, her uncle Tony molested her. This went on for three years, until Tony was locked up for attempted murder. If he hadn't gotten arrested, he would still be sexually abusing young Chasity.

During that time, Chasity tried to tell her mother about her Uncle Tony, but she dismissed her daughter as a liar.

"Stop lying on my brother! You know damn well he didn't do anything to your little nasty ass!" her mother stated.

"I'm not lying! Every night he sneaks into my room and he rapes me! And you don't believe me! Why would I make that up?" Chasity would plead with her mother to stop Tony, to no avail.

Right now, Chasity needed a drink just thinking about her uncle Tony. Her body shook as if she were about to have a stroke.

Detective Colon stopped the recorder. "Are you all right?" she asked. "I'm sorry to hear what happened to you."

"It's okay, I needed to get it out. I've only told two people, that's my mother and now you." Chasity stared directly into Detective Colon's brown eyes.

"So, can you skip to the part where you met Torian? How did you meet Torian Berk?" Detective Colon pressed the record button again, certain her lie would come within the next three minutes.

****

There was no alcohol in the condo, so Chasity took a ride to the liquor store to get her favorite, Hennessy. She decided to go to the liquor store in the hood to stunt in her new BMW.

When she pulled up, eight Black men were standing in front of the store selling drugs. Everyone in her neighborhood knew her, so heads turned when she pulled up in the new whip.

Her weed supplier, Sincere, was one of the eight men standing in front of the store. He was the first to approach her.

"What's up, Cherry? Who's BMW?" Sincere asked.

"Mine," she responded.

"Yeah right, and I'm President Obama."

"Whatever, Sincere. You know I don't be fronting, you better act like you know!" Chasity was feeling herself.

"Okay, you moving up in the world!"

"Something like that."

She exited the car and entered the liquor store, grabbing the biggest bottle of Henny they had. Once she made her purchase, she walked out to her car. A gentleman pulled up next to her in a BMW just like hers, but it was white with 22-inch rims. She studied the car with admiration. Then she glanced at the driver and was immediately attracted to him and vice versa. *This nigga is fly as hell.*

"Nice car," he said.

"Yours is better. I like your rims," she responded.

"I can get chrome rims for the low at my boys shop."

"How much?" she asked.

"About $2,600 for something like these."

"Okay, that's a good price."

"Take my number. My name is Torian. Lock me in." He winked.

"I most definitely will. I'm calling you now. My name is Cherry."

"Okay, Cherry. I look forward to hearing from you."

"No doubt, Torian. You will hear from me this week."

Chasity watched Torian walk into the bodega. Torian was one of the most handsome guys she'd seen in a while. She didn't get open that easily, but she was a sucker for a pretty face. And Torian had that and a muscular body to match.

I wonder what he does for a living. Whatever it is, he's getting money!

Her ringing cell phone brought her out of her thoughts.

"Hello?" she said in an annoying tone.

"It's me. Vinny. Where are you?"

"I went to the liquor store."

"I almost panicked when I woke up and you weren't there."

Sounds like a stalker now, Chasity thought.

"No need to panic. I'm not going nowhere." She pictured Torian in her head. "I'm on my way back to the condo now."

"Okay, see you in a minute."

She hung up.

One thing Cherry hated was to feel smothered by a man. She would deal with it because of the car and the condo, but she had to lay down some rules and boundaries. She knew how to play him. *He's like silly putty in my hand.*

What was most on her mind was Torian. She already liked him, and all they had was a brief conversation. Torian was the type of man she could see herself in a committed relationship with. Her one and only serious relationship had been with a man named Benji, who'd broken her heart by messing with her best friend. Ever since then, Chasity vowed to never fall in love again. With Torian, falling in love wasn't a real concern for her. Although she was highly physically attracted to him, she was nobody's fool. But then again, that's how it all starts, with the physical. Next thing you know you're in love.

When she got back to the condo, Vinny was lying on the bed watching the TV show *Cops*.

"I hate that show," she said, entering the bedroom.

"I can change it. I watch it 'cause my—" Vinny stopped mid-sentence and changed the subject. "I missed you."

"What were you about to say?" she asked, noticing the quick change of topic.

"Nothing. My brother is a cop, that's why I watch this show."

"Your brother is a pig?"

"Yes, he's a pig."

Chasity went to the bathroom as nature called. Vinny opened the door while she was sitting on the toilet to tell her something and she lost it.

"Damn! Can I go to the bathroom in peace?" she yelled.

"I'm sorry, babe." He quickly shut the door.

She finished using the bathroom and stormed out, putting one hand on her hip before addressing him.

"Listen, I'm going to have to lay down some ground rules. First of all, I don't like *no* man that needs to know where I am at all times, like I'm on parole or something. Second, when I go to the bathroom, that's the only place in this condo that I want to go alone. That's one of my biggest pet peeves."

"Okay, I'm sorry babe. I'll never do it again. And I'll try to not treat you like you're on parole. You're funny."

Same thing that can make you laugh can make you cry.

For some reason just then, Vinny repulsed her. Chasity looked at his short, fat appearance and frowned. His dress code wasn't what she liked. He wore black slacks and a white button up that was too tight. She failed abundantly at even trying to hide her expression.

"Babe, are you all right?" Vinny asked, noticing her countenance.

Chasity shook her head no. "I'm just not feeling good right now. I think I'm getting my period," she lied, needing an excuse for the moment.

"I'm going to give you a little space for a couple of days. Is that okay?"

"That's fine, baby." She kissed him on his forehead. "I'm sorry if I made you feel unwanted. It's not that. I just gotta have my personal time, that's all."

"It's okay. I understand." Vinny moped his way toward the door. "I'll see you in a couple of days." He turned back with his mouth downturned and eyes full of sadness. "See you later."

Getting no response, Vinny walked out the door, hoping he hadn't pushed her too far away.

Chasity wanted to laugh. *Pitiful.* She felt no sympathy for Vinny. Nothing made her happier than not having to see him for two days.

As soon as Vinny was gone, she called Torian.

"Hello?" he answered on the first ring.

"Hey Torian."

"What's up, Cherry?"

"I was wondering if you wanted to hang out with me tonight."

"Of course. Where you want to meet?"

A cop opened the interrogation room door, interrupting Chasity's recorded interview. "Detective Colon, Lieutenant Hank wants to see you in his office for a minute."

"Excuse me, I'll be right back." Detective Colon got up and left the room. *Sonofabitch!*

****

Furious about the interruption, Detective Colon stormed into Lieutenant Hank's office and slammed the door. .

"What the hell was that, Lieutenant? She was almost about to tell me what I needed to know!" Detective Colon was fuming as she spoke.

"Who the *hell* do you think you're talking to, Detective!" he fired back with venom in his tone, which caused Detective Colon to calm down. "Listen, I can't have you doing this. It's against the department's policy," Lieutenant Hanks said sternly.

"I know . . . I just want to know. Aren't I entitled to know, considering the circumstances?"

"I'll give you thirty more minutes and that's it! Now go and make the most of it."

Detective Colon walked back to the interrogation room, closed her eyes and sighed before entering.

"Where were we?"

She pressed record, ready to steal more testimony from Chasity "Cherry" Johnson. Detective Colon wasn't sure what she'd do with the information once they got down to the specifics.

Little did Chasity know, whatever she revealed from this point on could end her life, or save it. Detective Colon needed enough evidence to pin any charge on Chasity for her involvement in this double homicide.

AMERICAN D - BOY

Detective Colon had a personal vendetta. Chasity was her target.

VENOM IN MY VEINZ

A NOVEL BY

RUMONT TEKAY

Wahida Clark Presents
Butterfly
A Novel By
Michael A. Robinson